More Praise for *An Ornithologist's Guide to Life*

"I've been reading and writing for around 65 years now, and how can it be that I've never read anything by—or even heard of—somebody as wonderful as Ann Hood? . . . *An Ornithologist's Guide to Life* is . . . an antidote to the vulgarity, love-of-violence and bone-dumb stupidity we tend to encounter every day. . . . These tales are unpretentious, sometimes funny, sometimes heartbreaking, but all written from a position of tenderness so profound that at any moment, on any page, feeling bursts, explodes, into painful knowledge or knowledgeable pain."

—Carolyn See, *Washington Post*

"Humorous, heartfelt stories. . . . [Hood's] quirky characterization, stylistic intelligence, and adroit timing combine to produce an ending that the reader feels in the gut. . . . A strong, fine collection overall."   —*Kirkus Reviews*

"[Hood] takes direct aim at failed relationships, sexual betrayals and encounters, death, family secrets, loss, and sudden, often incandescent epiphanies with a deceptively frank and luminous style that sensationalizes nothing but quietly strips away the layers of her troubled and stranded characters. . . . These beautiful tales resonate and shimmer and in their realistic way reveal the way we live now."

—Sam Coale, *Providence Journal*

"Hood's tales are sexy, silly and full of sympathy for trapped creatures of the feathered or human variety."

—*Time Out New York*

"Hood, author of *Somewhere Off the Coast of Maine*, has an easy, natural voice and a beguiling sense of humor. It's easy to slip into the intriguing situations of the stories in her latest collection, *An Ornithologist's Guide to Life*."

—Margaret Quamme, *Columbus Dispatch*

"These stories are simply the way life is, not the way we would like it to be, and reading them is joyous, painful and, finally, exhilarating."

—Susan Larson, *New Orleans Times-Picayune*

"Ann Hood tells 11 sharp, surreal stories in her new collection, *An Ornithologist's Guide to Life*."   —*More*

"Short stories are sorely underrated, yet they are a wonderful amuse bouche between headier works or as a staple for commuters, and this new collection by acclaimed author Ann Hood will keep readers sated."   —*Elliot Bay Booknotes*

"Writing with elegant precision, Hood's awareness of place is tactile and familiar, drawing the reader into the scenes with her fumbling characters as they struggle with issues that require both courage and resilience; in the end, each tale uncovers an irrevocable moment of reckoning. . . . As the title intimates, the author is indeed an observer of human behavior, in this case human, not winged. Her protagonists are skillfully arranged for maximum emotional impact, illuminated, exposing the fragile undersides they are vainly trying to protect."

—*curled up with a good book*

"These stories have bite. . . . Hood has enough perception to leave her characters room to grow after the stories end."
—*Library Journal*

"An entertaining, brightly detailed collection."
—Kathryn Schwille, *Charlotte Observer*

"Ann Hood has written a moving collection of stories about our everyday victories and defeats. Diverse and filled with surprises, these stories are bound by a common vision and with characters, lovingly drawn, who come together in incongruous and unanticipated ways."
—Mary Morris, author of *Acts of God*

"Of course there is humor and wisdom and grace in these well-crafted short stories—Ann Hood wrote them. Even in the face of adversity, her characters cannot help but revel in all that life has to offer; they know no other tack."
—Helen Schulman, author of *P.S.*

"What's possible after loss? Ann Hood's stories aim to find out by tracing the lives of families and couples blown apart by divorce, death, abandonment, and other departures. What's left? Pain, tenuous new attachments, and hope, all of which Hood explores in her energetic new collection. Wry, entertaining, and entirely of the moment, *An Ornithologist's Guide to Life* offers up honest examples of how people in the twenty-first century manage to carry on."
—Debra Spark, author of *The Ghost of Bridgetown*

"Ann Hood's writing is an unusual combination of the delicate and the fierce. The stories in her collection feature characters whose lives are as eccentric, imperfect, and mysterious as our own. *An Ornithologist's Guide to Life* is one of those collections that is a pure pleasure to dip into, for its author has so much to say, and we really want to listen."
　　　　　　　　　—Meg Wolitzer, author of *Surrender, Dorothy*

"Winging her way through caverns, kitchens, tattoo parlors, and tourist destinations, Ann Hood blesses with extraordinarism the most ordinary inhabitants of our world, proving yet again she is a rare literary bird who should be on the life list of every reader, and writer."　　—Suzanne Strempek Shea, author of *Songs from a Lead-Lined Room*

ALSO BY ANN HOOD

Somewhere Off the Coast of Maine

Waiting to Vanish

Three Legged Horse

Something Blue

Places to Stay the Night

The Properties of Water

Ruby

Do Not Go Gentle

—— ANN HOOD ——

W. W. NORTON & COMPANY
New York London

An

ORNITHOLOGIST'S
GUIDE *to* LIFE

These stories have appeared in:

Total Cave Darkness, *The Paris Review*; The Rightness
of Things, *Five Points*; The Language of Sorrow, *Five
Points*; After Zane, *Redbook*; Joelle's Mother, *Good
Housekeeping*; Escapes, *Story*; Lost Parts, *The Colorado
Review*; Dropping Bombs, *GlimmerTrain*; Inside
Gorbachev's Head, *The Colorado Review*; New People,
Gulf Coast Quarterly; An Ornithologist's Guide to
Life, *GlimmerTrain*.

For information about permission to reproduce
selections from this book, write to Permissions,
W. W. Norton & Company, Inc., 500 Fifth Avenue,
New York, NY 10110

Manufacturing by The Haddon Craftsmen, Inc.
Book design by Judith Stagnitto Abbate
Production Manager: Anna Oler

Library of Congress Cataloging-in-Publication Data
Hood, Ann, 1956–
An ornithologist's guide to life / Ann Hood.—1st ed.
p. cm.
ISBN 0-393-05900-6
1. United States—Social life and customs—Fiction.
2. Psychological fiction, American. I. Title.
PS3558.0537075 2004
813'.54—dc22   2004006112

ISBN 0-393-32704-3 pbk.

W. W. Norton & Company, Inc.
500 Fifth Avenue, New York, N.Y. 10110
www.wwnorton.com

W. W. Norton & Company Ltd.
Castle House, 75/76 Wells Street, London W1T 3QT

1 2 3 4 5 6 7 8 9 0

In loving memory of my daughter Gracie Belle

September 24, 1996–April 18, 2002

CONTENTS

ACKNOWLEDGMENTS

THE AUTHOR WISHES to thank the Providence Area Writing Group for their comments and suggestions on many of these stories; the editors of the various journals and magazines where the stories first appeared; Yaddo; Marianne Merola and Meg Giles; Gail Hochman; Jill Bialosky; Gloria Hood; Melissa Hood; my husband, Lorne Adrain; and our son, Sam, whose love gives me strength.

An

ORNITHOLOGIST'S

GUIDE *to* LIFE

TOTAL CAVE DARKNESS

HE CALLS HER Sweetheart, Darling, Honey Pie. Martha calls him Reverend. Even now, as she watches him stretch out on the hood of his car, shirtless, smiling to himself, face turned toward the blistering July sun, Martha thinks: The Reverend is so damn young. The pay phone is hot against her ear and she smells someone else's bad breath emanating from it. Martha is sweaty from heat and humidity, sore from too much acrobatic sex. And she wants a drink. God help her, she wants a cold beer, a chilled white wine, a vodka and tonic. Anything.

Six hundred miles from this parking lot, Martha's mother answers the phone with a weary hello. Massachusetts is in the middle of a heat wave too. Martha knows this. In between sex and free HBO she watches the Weather Channel. The whole country is hot.

"It's me," Martha says with forced cheerfulness. "I'm about to go into a cave so I figured I should check in, in case you never hear from me again. You know."

Her mother lowers her voice as if the phone could be tapped. "A cave! Is that all you have to say for yourself?"

Then there is a silence in which Martha hears her mother

thinking: You have done crazy things in your day, but running off with a priest tops them all.

The Reverend lazily wipes the sweat from his forehead with the back of his hand. He is nine years younger than Martha, with startling green eyes that remind her of her childhood cat Boo and a body that must come from God himself: wide shouldered and strong and golden haired.

"He's not a priest, you know, Mom. He's a minister. A Protestant."

The Reverend scratches his balls with another lazy motion and Martha looks away.

"What did I say? Did I say anything about it? I don't care what you call him," her mother is saying. "He wears one of those little white collars, doesn't he? He gets up on Sunday mornings and preaches to people, doesn't he?"

Martha smiles at this. Today is Sunday, and when he got up with her this morning he was definitely not preaching. Although she had jokingly whispered amen when they were done.

"What are you thinking?" her mother says. "You're a grown woman, Martha. Over forty—"

"Just over forty," Martha reminds her, feeling cross.

"And you take off with him for three weeks—"

"Two! Almost two."

"And everyone knows the two of you are not off praying together." Her mother's voice grows weary again as she repeats, "What are you thinking?"

Martha asks herself the same thing. She had been gripped by an urge to call home after all these days away as if this simple act of reaching out would make everything different. Instead, everything is exactly the same. Her mother's voice, baffled and questioning, sounds all too familiar. Words like *irresponsible* and *thoughtless* buzz around Martha's head like mosquitoes.

A bright yellow car pulls into the parking lot, and Martha squints at its unfamiliar license plate. She has been keeping a mental tally of all the different states' license plates she sees. South Dakota? Yes. The faces of the presidents are stamped right on the plate. There was a time, before the drinking took over so much of her life, when Martha could easily do things like name the presidents who were carved at Mount Rushmore or rattle off the state capitals without hesitation. But now her brain is all thick and soupy. She tells herself one more drink would not make it any worse.

As if he read her mind, the Reverend appears at her side and takes her hand as tenderly as an adolescent on a first date.

"Reverend Dave," Martha whispers.

He smiles at her with his even white teeth while her mother shrieks in her ear. "What? He's right there? Right this minute?"

The Reverend nuzzles her. So many things he does remind her of her Boo that sometimes Martha worries that she will fall in love with Reverend Dave. She thinks of how Boo used to wait for her to come from school, perched on the low hanging branch of a maple tree at the corner of her street. Sometimes Martha would stop and watch him there instead of turning the corner. She would count—one minute, two, three. No matter how late she was, Boo waited. As soon as he saw her, he'd jump from branch to fence to sidewalk, landing right at her feet.

Thinking of his loyalty and patience makes Martha say, "Oh."

"Martha?" her mother says, demanding, angry. "What is he doing?"

The Reverend lifts Martha's hand in his and presses her close, swaying against her body like they are at the prom. He is humming, off-key.

"Saving me," Martha tells her mother. "He's saving my life."

BACK IN MARCH, when Martha's drinking lost her everything—the condo in Marblehead that looked out over the harbor, her job as the restaurant/movie/theater critic for *The North Shore Press,* her husband—she moved in with her mother so she could drink in peace. "I've come to straighten out," Martha lied the day they dragged her boxes across her mother's powder blue wall-to-wall carpeting and into the guest room. Her mother had a condo too, in Swampscott. And a job. And a boyfriend. She wasn't happy to have Martha back. "I'm not the Betty Ford Clinic here," she grumbled. "You come back, you're on your own."

At first, Martha made a show of getting up with her mother every morning and having dry toast and lots of coffee. She circled ads for jobs in the classifieds in red marker and discussed the pros and cons of each one. Her mother frowned at her and shook her head, not disgusted as much as baffled. "Why don't you just take yourself to AA?" her mother said one morning before she left for her job in the Better Dresses department at Filene's. She wore a Donna Karan outfit that, with markdowns and her discount, she got for eighty-eight dollars. "AA?" Martha laughed. "I'm not that far gone. I just need to get my head on straight." After her mother left, Martha paced while first the talk shows and then the soap operas droned on behind her. Her mind skipped and flitted from one thing to the next, leaving her unable to complete anything or to concentrate on something as easy as the *Reader's Digest*s her mother kept in the bathroom.

But at five o'clock she was always able to focus. She turned off the television and went to the kitchen to fix a vodka and tonic in her mother's jumbo insulated to-go cup. She could nurse one of these until her mother came home and the two of them ate dinner together, sometimes joined by her mother's boyfriend Frankie. Martha always cleaned up afterward, then slipped out between *Wheel of Fortune* and *Jeopardy*. By eight o'clock she was settled on a stool at Matty's or the Landing, drinking until closing.

The truth was, Martha loved these nights. She loved the sound of ice cubes and laughter and jukebox music mingling together. She loved how her tongue felt thick in her mouth, how when she shifted her head too quickly the world around her spun. She loved the easy way a man might throw his arm around her shoulder, the first touch of a stranger's cold beery tongue on her body. She loved everything about drinking. All of it. For Martha, her favorite part of the day was quarter of five, watching the clock make its slow movement toward her first vodka, filling the glass with ice, then tonic, holding the bottle of vodka in her arms like a baby.

HER OLD FRIEND Patty, newly relocated to Chicago, her voice filled with so much happiness that Martha wished she would stop calling, ended each conversation by reminding Martha that help was out there, "when you're ready." Patty had been to AA, NA, OA, and every other A imaginable. "I like drinking," Martha told Patty. "So do I," Patty said, her voice righteous, smug. It was Patty who gave Martha the Reverend's number. She had described him as kind and helpful. "Also, very cute in a koala way," she said. Who would have imagined that Martha and the Reverend would run off together? That they would end up here in this parking lot in Virginia, about to go into the Endless Caverns? Certainly not Martha.

She reads to the Reverend about all the other caverns they drove past. "The Luray Caverns have an organ made out of stalagmites. The Skyline Caverns have cave flowers not found in any other caves in the U.S."

"Sweetheart," he says, grinning at her, "we missed all of those. We weren't thinking about caverns. Now we're thinking about them and we're here. That's how lucky we are. As soon as we imagine something that we want, we get it."

"Mel Gibson," Martha says, closing her eyes. But really she is imagining a bottle of vodka.

"Now don't go breaking my heart, darling," the Reverend whispers, holding her close.

He is a solid man, like a rock or a mountain in her arms. Martha keeps her eyes closed and tries to think of something other than the way the first swallow of alcohol tastes, how it burns a little, punches your gut, makes you swoon.

"There's no fairyland in there," Martha says. She is whispering too. "The Luray Caverns have Fairy Land. Reflecting pools that make the stalactites look like sand castles."

Reverend Dave steps away from her and laughs. "We

already know it's an illusion," he says. "Saved ourselves the trip! We've got the Endless Caverns. Miles and miles explored," he says, tapping the guidebook in her hand, "but no end ever found."

"What were we thinking to come here like this?" Martha says with a sigh.

They both know that she doesn't just mean here, to Virginia, to these caves, but rather the way they packed up his Dodge and drove out of town, meandering for almost two weeks now, sleeping at Motel 6s and eating breakfasts of 7-Eleven coffee and doughnuts. Every day they drive and drive, choosing their routes at random—he likes the name of a particular town, she wants to see something she'd heard about once, a lifetime ago. He has left behind a congregation of Unitarians who think he's spending his vacation in Michigan with his parents. She has left behind her longest lover—drinking. If she had not woken up one afternoon and realized that she had lost three whole days of her life—three days! she still thinks in amazement, and no matter how hard she tries she can not retrieve a single minute of them—she would still be at her mother's condo waiting for her first vodka of the day.

"Hey," the Reverend says, "it's been almost two weeks. You haven't had even one drop in two whole weeks."

"Some treatment you devised," Martha snaps because she wants a drink so bad that the mention of her meager accomplishment embarrasses her. "Take a drunk, withhold liquor, drive her around all day, and sleep with her every night. Wow. You might even get a write-up in *Cosmopolitan*. 'How I Cure Alcoholics' by Reverend Dave."

He looks so wounded that Martha almost reaches out to

touch his cheek. But instead she whirls around and marches across the parking lot on wobbly legs to the fireworks store. She expects him to follow her but he doesn't. Martha stands in the middle of the store, alone, surrounded by country hams and a dizzying array of fireworks.

"Do you sell . . . uh . . . like microbrewery beers? Something local?" she asks the woman at the cash register. Martha hopes she sounds like a tourist instead of like someone desperate for a drink.

The woman points to a cooler in the corner. "We got some from up in Maryland."

Martha's fingers tremble as she opens the cooler and lifts a beer from a six-pack carton. Its label is colorful, happy. Martha presses the cool amber bottle to her cheek.

The woman frowns. "You want just the one?"

She looks out at the parking lot, where the air ripples with heat and Reverend Dave kicks at stones, sending them flying past cars with license plates from Utah, Texas, Pennsylvania. Martha is flushed with guilt and excitement both. Like the winner on *Supermarket Sweepstakes* she begins to pull fireworks from the shelves around her, until she settles on a Roman candle and a box of sparklers.

"And these," Martha says.

THE REVEREND LOOKS like a little boy out there, kicking stones, sulking. Nine years between them is really a lot of years, Martha thinks, not for the first time. Last week they drove to a county fair somewhere in Pennsylvania to hear

Paul Revere and the Raiders. Reverend Dave had never heard of them, even after Martha sang "Let Me Take You Where the Action Is" to him naked in their motel room.

"I have no idea who they are," he told her, "but I'm sure I like your rendition better than theirs."

"I wanted to marry Mark Lindsay," she said. When he shrugged, she added, "Their lead singer."

Even though the Reverend had danced with her, the Swim and the Jerk and the Twist, not one of their songs was remotely familiar to him. He had looked like a child, jumping up and down beside her, his hair flopping into his eyes. When they'd sung a ballad, "Hungry," he took Martha into his bearish grasp and danced close and slow, smoothing her hair and not at all childlike.

"Nine years," she whispers. "It's too much." But then she remembers something: back at the pay phone, the song he was humming—it was "Hungry." And this small gesture from him sends her running toward him.

"I got fireworks!" she yells.

He looks up, and what she sees in his eyes almost breaks her heart. The Reverend has fallen in love with her. She doesn't know whether to turn and run the other way or keep going into his open arms. What she does is stop, a few feet from him, and hold up the bag.

"Sparklers and everything," she says. She imagines the beer bottle nestled among all the explosives, everything ticking away, ready to go off at any minute.

"We can light them later," she says.

Reverend Dave nods and begins to walk toward the caverns. Knowing the beer is so close—that after the tour she can duck into the ladies' room and drink it down, or later back at the motel while he's in the shower—just having it makes Martha feel lighthearted.

"I'm sorry I was so mean," she tells him.

"I know," he says.

ON THE FOURTH of July they found themselves in Gettysburg, unable to get a room.

"'Cause of the reenactment," the fifth motel clerk told them.

Finally they found a room at an inn where everyone dressed in period costumes: women in long dresses and bonnets, the men in blue and gray uniforms. It depressed Martha. Their canopy bed and braided rug and the pitcher on the bureau, all of it made her sad.

"No HBO," she told the Reverend as she flicked through the channels. She settled on the Weather Channel and watched the heat spread across the country, relentless.

The Reverend came up behind her and hugged her around the waist. Outside they could hear cannons being fired, and muskets.

"Why do you do it?" he asked her. It was the first time since she'd walked into his office at the church back in May that he asked her that.

"I can't remember," she'd said, which was the truth. "But I love it more than anything. It is what I love."

"I don't believe it's all you will ever love." He turned her around to face him, but she averted her eyes. "I think you could love a person," he said. "The right person."

Martha looked up at him and laughed. The smell of gunpowder filled the room. "Like a reverend? Like someone practically a decade younger than me?"

"Yes," he said simply. Then he kissed her full on the lips.

Later, naked in the canopy bed, Martha propped herself on one elbow to look down at him. That day she'd walked into his office he'd had on khaki shorts and a Hawaiian shirt. She had studied him closely then too, like she was now. His face was round, boyish. That day in his office she'd said, "You're the reverend here?" And then she had burst into tears. Later, she had told him about those missing days, days when she could have run over someone, gotten AIDS, done anything—"God knows what," she'd said, and he'd burst out laughing. "Sorry," he told her, "me being a minister and all, the God thing struck me as funny." She wasn't sure what to make of him. Not then nor weeks later when he took her to a corny Italian restaurant and paid the roaming accordian player to sing "That's Amore" to her.

"You courted me," Martha whispered from her side of the canopy bed.

Even though his eyes were closed he smiled.

"I came in every day just so I wouldn't drink, and you let me sit there in your office week after week until one day you said—"

Reverend Dave opened his eyes. "'Let me buy you dinner.' And you said yes." He was playing with her hair, wrapping pieces of it in his fingers, then letting it fall free. "I never did that before. Asked out someone who came to me for help."

"Sure. I bet that's what you say to all the drunk forty-year-olds who've fucked up their lives. It helps to make them feel special."

The Reverend pulled her close to him by the hair.

"Hey," Martha said.

"Shut up," he told her. "You don't know anything."

He had told her that he was supposed to visit his family in Grand Rapids during his three weeks off.

"For all you care I could have gone to Michigan and left you behind."

"I know this," Martha said, keeping her hair tangled in his hand. "I know I hate this town and all this morbid history. I know I want to go downstairs to Ye Olde Tavern and have a drink. I know more than you think I do."

"Shut up," he said again. He was kissing her, leaving her no choice.

THEIR TOUR GUIDE is a teenager named Stuart. He has Buddy Holly glasses pus-filled pimples and a deep voice that Martha is certain belongs to someone else. Every time he talks he startles her. Reverend Dave keeps asking questions about oxygen and bats and spelunking, but Martha is having trouble listening. The cave looks fake, like the backdrop for a movie or the re-created environments at zoos. When no one is looking, Martha touches the stalagmites, knocks them with her knuckles as if she can prove them false.

"We're in the cut-rate cavern," Martha whispers to the Reverend. "We missed all the good ones."

He steps away from her. He has not forgiven her for what she said back in the parking lot. All it would take is a touch or a kiss, and she would have him back again. Martha stays away. She pretends she is part of a family from Georgia who knows all the answers to Stuart's stupid questions. She is certain the family has been here before and so technically they are cheating when they shout out the answers. Still, they act smug.

"Have you been to Luray?" Martha asks the mother. They are making their way through a long tunnel. The Reverend's red-flowered shirt disappears around a corner.

"They're really commercial," the mother tells Martha. "We like Endless best."

Up close Martha sees that the woman is probably the same age as the Reverend.

"Your husband's real cute," the woman whispers. "Is he really a minister?"

Husband? Martha thinks. Her heart is beating too fast and all she can do is nod.

"Golly, our minister is an old fart with a gut out to here."

"He's nine years younger than me," Martha blurts.

The woman looks pleased rather than appalled. "Good for you!" she says.

They reach the place where Stuart told them to wait for him. He is talking now about rivers in the caves but Martha could care less. The Reverend has his head bent, leaning toward Stuart, gobbling up all this useless information. Like at Gettysburg, where he had to stop at the visitors' center and get brochures before they left. Then he kept reading to her from them. The next night, in bed, he'd recited the Gettysburg Address from memory in the voice she guessed he used for preaching. Remembering this, Martha feels a pang of something from long ago. A feeling that she cannot name. Unexpectedly, she thinks of Boo and how he used to wrap himself around her neck like a stole.

Martha moves closer to the Reverend, but he doesn't look at her. Everyone is looking up at the ceiling.

"Many people see the face of Jesus there," Stuart says in his deep voice.

Almost everyone is saying ah, and pointing.

Martha clutches the bag of fireworks in her hands. Despite the colder weather down here in the cave, her hands are sweating. When she presses the bag close to her chest she feels the cool hard bottle inside.

Reverend Dave is looking up too. Martha follows his gaze and tries hard to see the face of Jesus, but there is just more of the fake rock. This morning at the motel, the Reverend ran out of the bathroom, naked and wet, took Martha by the hand, and brought her to the small sliver of window by the shower. "Look! " he said, awed. Martha had to stand on tiptoe to see.

"What?" she said.

The Reverend put his hands around her waist and lifted her so that she could see. Framed like a small painting were the Blue Ridge Mountains and the rolling hills below them. In the early morning mist, they seemed wrapped in gauze.

"Isn't that one of the most beautiful things you've ever seen, honey pie?" he said in a soft voice, holding her there in place so that she was forced to look.

Martha squirmed out of his grasp. "I like the view from the bedroom better. Parking lot, strip mall, ribbon of high-way." She'd hoped he would know that she stole that phrase—*ribbon of highway*—from Woody Guthrie.

Now Martha stares hard at the spot where Stuart is shin-ing his flashlight. She doesn't want to make another wisecrack; she wants desperately to find something there. But before she has a chance, Stuart says, "Total cave darkness," and turns off the light. They are left in a dark that is so thick, Martha cannot see the fingers she holds up to her own eyes. She finds herself leaning into the darkness. The bag she has been holding drops, and in the stillness there comes the shattering of the bottle and the yeasty smell of the beer.

"Oops," someone says, and the group titters.

"In total cave darkness," Stuart booms—like God, Martha decides, "you would go blind and crazy in just two weeks."

Martha wants the lights on again. She wants to find a face in the cave ceiling. She is certain if given another chance she will see it. In the darkness, she reaches out, not certain what she will find. Through the beer and the musty cave smell, Martha smells the Reverend beside her. Until this instant she did not know she could recognize his scent. And then her hand finds his, warm and familiar. Martha cranes her neck and lifts her face upward. There is something there, she decides. The longer she stands like this, squeezing the Reverend's hand and staring into the total cave darkness, the more that something begins to take shape. It is the blurry face of a stranger in a bar, promising her vodka if she will go home with him. It is the back of his New England Patriots sweatshirt as she stumbles across the parking lot toward his car, gagging on the smell of fresh sea air. She remembers peeling paint, sour sheets, a stranger's body. She remembers that for three days last spring she did anything for her next drink.

Without warning, the lights come back on. They all squint at each other in the brightness. Martha sees the Reverend looking at her.

"Or maybe you like the darkness better?" Stuart asks, grinning. He snaps off the lights again.

Someone behind Martha gasps. But instead of panicking her, the darkness wraps itself around Martha and soothes her. It is as if she is falling, like the game she played as a child where you fall backward, hoping someone will be there to catch you.

THE RIGHTNESS

OF THINGS

———————————

EVERY TIME RACHEL sees Mary, she is struck by how alike the two of them are—the same strawberry blond hair, the same parade of freckles across their arms and cheeks, even the same old wire-rimmed glasses, round ones that have bent over time and look slightly outdated; people often mistake them for sisters. Chasing Sofia up the steps to Mary's house, Rachel considers this, the way they seem so alike, so close, but after five years of friendship, Rachel still feels slightly awkward coming here, to Mary's house.

The house is a large Victorian, perfectly restored. It is a pleasant shade of pink, with a darker pink gingerbread trim. Inside, the rooms are dark and cool, the floors covered with Oriental rugs, the kitchen cupboards filled with the things one accumulates in married life—wedding gift soup tureens and espresso cups and parfait glasses, crystal vases that will be filled on Valentine's Day and anniversaries, good china.

Perhaps that is what causes the feeling, Rachel thinks.

Ever since her divorce three years ago, she and Sofia have lived on the top floor of a three family house in the iffier part of the city. In summer, now, the apartment is too hot and stuffy and Rachel imagines she can smell the remnants of every meal she has ever cooked there. They have no yard. Sofia's room is too small to contain all the things a five-year-old needs, so that her dollhouse and play stove and drawing easel crowd the living room and kitchen.

Rachel hears Mary approaching; it always takes her a long time to answer the door. She will have been in the basement folding clothes, or upstairs braiding her daughter's hair, or elbow deep in bread dough.

"Look at me, Sofia," Rachel whispers.

Sofia looks up at her with red Kool-Aid rimmed lips. Her sweaty round face, dark eyes, tangled curls, break Rachel's heart. She finds herself still angry at Peter for doing something as foolish and cliché as falling in love with his assistant. She finds herself angry at herself too. Three years later and she still has not found the right job, a better home, a new love.

The door creaks open, and there stands Mary—yes, it was bread she was making; there is flour on her shirt and in her hair—and *her* Sophia. It was what had brought them together in the first place: their daughters had the same name, though spelled differently, they later discovered. But that day in the supermarket—a day as hot as this one; Rachel had gone simply to cool off—when Mary had cooed to her daughter, *Sophia, Sophia, you're so good today,* Rachel had blurted, *Why, I have a Sofia too!* and she'd pointed at her daughter, who was crushing a pint of strawberries, one by one. That was the summer Peter had moved out, the summer Sofia had meningitis and was in the hospital for two weeks, the summer that Rachel thought of as the time when everything changed.

But Mary is ushering them into the house, and stands in the foyer calling, "Sophia! They're here!"

There is the smell of burned candles, the hushed air, the stream of light spilling through the stained glass window that presides over the house's impressive double staircase. Rachel thinks of church.

"Can I go up?" Sofia asks. Her voice is hushed too, awed, as it always is when they enter Mary's house. She holds on to Rachel's clammy hand.

Mary smiles down at her. "Yes. Of course. Run right up."

Upstairs Sophia has her own playroom, with dolls lined up on shelves and a small table always set up for a tea party.

Rachel thinks Mary looks too pink, flushed, perhaps. She is Italian, but fair, and her skin burns too easily in the sun. When she gardens, she wears long sleeves, an oversized straw hat. Rachel has seen her like that, working in her garden. *I like to make things grow,* Mary has told her. She has given Rachel shoots from her plants, small pots of herbs for her windowsill, but Rachel cannot make anything thrive. Her houseplants refuse to flourish, even with expensive potting soil, careful attention, love.

"Have you been gardening?" Rachel asks, following Mary through her maze of rooms—the formal living room, the family room, the library, the pantry, and then finally, the kitchen.

"Not today," Mary says. "Too hot."

The kitchen is overly bright, a sunshine yellow that Mary has told Rachel was common in Victorians. But it reminds Rachel of her own old dorm room. She and her roommate had painted the cinderblock walls a similar yellow with bright orange trim and put Indian bedspreads on their beds. When they got stoned at night, the room seemed to vibrate. It made them think of sunsets.

Mary pours two tall glasses of iced tea, and points to the bread cooling on the counter.

"I thought it would be ready by the time you got here but I'm moving so slowly," she says.

Rachel laughs. They both know that Mary always gets everything done. She goes to church. She gives dinner parties. She works out every day.

"Right," Rachel says. "Slow for you is still high speed for the rest of us."

Mary leans toward Rachel, conspiratorially. "No," she says, lowering her voice. "I *am* slow. You'll never guess."

Rachel shrugs, smiles. Mary often has announcements. She and Dan are going to India, or she's heading a clothing drive for children's winter coats, or Sophia is going to a certain private school. She shares all of this information like it's top secret, as if Rachel is the only one she's divulging the information to.

"What?" Rachel says. The tea has fresh mint in it.

"I'm *pregnant*," Mary says, squeezing Rachel's arm with both of her cold, dry hands.

"Pregnant?" Rachel repeats, and her own stomach does a strange flop.

"Fourteen weeks," Mary tells her.

It comes back to Rachel, how in pregnancy time is counted week by week. It takes her a moment to calculate.

"Why, that's over three months!" Rachel says finally.

Mary's face clouds. "Don't be mad," she says, still gripping Rachel's arm. "I would have told you sooner, but I felt so superstitious. It's silly, I suppose. But we've been trying for two years—"

"You have?" Rachel asks, startled. Of course Mary wouldn't have told her that; they really aren't good enough friends for such an intimacy. Rachel used to refer to Mary as one of her "Mommy friends," the women she saw for play dates or in the playground or at Story Hour at the local bookstore. With her other friends, the ones she often thought of as her *real* friends, she sometimes made fun of the other mothers, their competitiveness, their ability to discuss trivial things endlessly. With her real friends, Rachel drank wine and rented foreign movies and stayed up too late; with her Mommy friends she put on a different, more placid face.

Somehow, she supposed, watching Mary's concerned expression, Mary fell somewhere in between.

"You *are* angry," Mary is saying. "It was silly of me to not tell you sooner. I just didn't want to jinx it, that's all."

"I was the same way," Rachel lies. "With Sofia. I waited forever to tell people."

Really she called everyone, immediately. She can still remember staring at the bright pink circle on the home pregnancy test while she dialed the phone. But Mary looks relieved.

"I just didn't want to jinx it," she says again. "You hear so many stories." Her face softens. "I'm so glad you're not mad at me," she says.

IT IS PETER'S weekend to have Sofia. These Fridays leave Rachel with such a mixed feeling—glad to have some time to herself, but jealous too, of all the hours he will have with Sofia. Packing her daughter's *Little Mermaid* suitcase, folding the baby doll pajamas, and tucking her Madeline doll in the zipper compartment, Rachel knows that it is not just the hours Peter will have with their daughter; it's the hours Yvonne will have. When Peter left them and moved in with Yvonne, everyone told Rachel it would never last. *He'll be back,* they assured her. But now, three years later, Peter and Yvonne are still together, cozily ensconced in a cottage at the beach.

Although Rachel has never been there, she imagines it every time Sofia drives off with them for the weekend. Weathered shingles, dark green shutters, Adirondack chairs overlooking the water. Some of these details she's gleaned from Sofia, or the dozens of pictures Yvonne and Peter take and send home with her. Others she makes up—sheer curtains, a clawfoot tub, botanical prints. And of course the animals. Sofia talks about them by name. *Lulu Gus Annabelle Rusty MacNamara Beatrice Bubba.* But Rachel gives them faces, breeds. She imagines two tabby cats, an Irish setter, several mutts, and a pair of cockatiels. Peter is a veterinarian, and he cannot resist a hurt or homeless animal. The one thing Rachel does not miss about her marriage is all the hours nursing strays, making splints for bunnies, or cleaning wounds. She lost an Afghan to blindness, a cat to feline leukemia, several dogs to hit and runs. It was too much. Now, she and Sofia keep goldfish. When one dies, they unceremoniously flush it down the toilet and go and buy a new one. Rachel likes that. You don't invest emotion in goldfish.

Outside, a horn beeps.

Rachel looks down the three stories to the street below, where Peter and Yvonne sit in his blue Honda, the same one he and Rachel picked out when she was pregnant with Sofia. It was reliable, they thought. Sensible. A good family car.

Sofia runs in to get her suitcase.

"Did you forget Madeline?" she asks. She stands on tip-toe and peeks out the window too.

"No," Rachel says, snippy. She has never forgotten to pack the doll, yet Sofia asks her every time.

Sofia swoops her suitcase from the bed, and begins to skip away.

"We're going for chowder and clamcakes," she says, grinning.

Her hair needs to be combed again, Rachel notices. And there is a spot of something bright blue in the middle of her Simba tee shirt. She will come back neater, bathed and sham-pooed with expensive beauty products made from papaya and mango and coconut. After her last weekend there, she returned with a white rope bracelet that she has refused to take off her wrist, even though it grows dingier every day.

"Have fun," Rachel says, trying to sound cheerful.

Sofia hesitates, frowning in the doorway.

The horn beeps again.

Sofia runs back into the room and hugs Rachel around the legs, hard, so that she is thrown slightly off balance.

"See you Sunday!" Sofia shouts, gone that fast.

Rachel turns back to the window. In a few seconds, Sofia appears, skipping again, across the front yard, a sad lot of dirt and tufts of brownish grass that remind Rachel of an old man's head.

"Daddy!" Sofia is shouting, happily.

Rachel's stomach tightens. Peter gets out of the car and picks Sofia up into his arms, bear hugs her, spinning slightly.

Sofia's thin legs wrap around her father's waist. Rachel sees the bottoms of her Keds as the two of them twirl. She sees the bright blond—*dyed,* her friends had assured her—of Yvonne's hair. She wants to turn away; there are things to get done. But behind her the house hums with quiet, and Rachel finds she cannot move from her spot at the window.

RACHEL HAS CONVINCED herself it is not a date. It is just dinner at Mary and Dan's.

"I've never fixed anyone up before," Mary told her on the phone that next morning, Saturday. "So I can't say that's what this is. But Dan's cousin Harry is coming over for dinner tonight and he was supposed to bring Victoria, his girlfriend, well, his *ex*-girlfriend, I guess, because he called fifteen minutes ago and said they've broken up but could he come anyway. And Dan and I immediately had the same thought: *Rachel.*" She paused, then added, "He's an architect."

Rachel was nursing a hangover; she'd had too much white wine the night before while she'd watched *Four Weddings and a Funeral,* a stupid movie to rent on a night when you've pulled out your own wedding album and cried over it.

Dressing for dinner, Rachel blames that early morning hangover for making her agree to go to Mary's. She hardly knows Dan; she has been single ever since she met Mary and, politely, Mary doesn't usually invite Rachel to couples' things. At Sophia's birthday parties, he is always there, grinning behind the video camera, handing out little Cinderella napkins and paper plates, pouring lemonade. But Rachel can hardly say she knows him. Tonight seems like one of those lines that she and Mary do not cross. On weekends, they don't even speak on the phone, never mind having dinner together.

But she is too cotton headed and embarrassed to cancel.

So she puts on her black cotton sheath, what she thinks of as her summer date dress, and black strappy sandals, and, because there is finally at least a breeze, she decides to walk to Mary's. Once she leaves her own neighborhood, with the clusters of tough looking teenagers on the corners and the loud music spilling from open windows, she actually enjoys the walk. She has brought a bottle of wine that her last date brought to her, a good wine that she's been saving for something special, and she cradles it in her arms as she meanders through the streets of Providence, walking slowly now that she's in the better part of town.

The houses here are large, like Mary's, with yards that have green grass, flower beds, neat hedges. When she can, she looks into the windows. There is a family eating dinner, an old man alone reading a book, the blue glare of a television. She should have been a spy, Rachel decides. Or something where she could watch things unnoticed. In college, she sat at the periphery of war protests, attending more for the free drugs that always got passed around. She remembers watching Peter and Sofia yesterday. Yes, she decides, she is a good voyeur.

Since her divorce, she has worked as a manager for various stores—books, shoes, and now an upscale toy store. She is ready to leave that job; it annoys her. All the overpriced wooden trains and planes, the complicated puzzles, the precious dolls that live behind glass. She did get Sofia's Madeline doll there, thirty percent off with her employee discount, but no other good has come from this job. In her mind, before she goes to sleep, Rachel tries to imagine what she will do next. But she majored in sociology, and never went on for her MSW. She is not trained for anything really. As crazy as it sounds, Rachel believed she would stay married to Peter, have children with him, grow old like that. She believed she would volunteer for good causes, help out in a soup kitchen, have friends over for good vegetarian meals from recipes in *Laurel's Kitchen*. In a way, she supposes as she turns down Mary's street of renovated Victorians, a street that seems to rocket you back in time, she had imagined she'd have a life not unlike Mary's.

The thought unsettles her, so that she is awkward again as she climbs the front steps and rings Mary's doorbell.

Rachel is surprised when Dan answers the door. She has come to think of the house as just Mary's. This too tall man with the slightly basset hound face startles her, as if he is the one who doesn't belong there.

"Finally," he says.

"Am I late?" Rachel asks, surprised.

The stained glass window looks ominous in this light. Rachel cannot remember ever being here at night before. She shivers.

"Just twenty minutes," he says, sounding cheerful. But Rachel recalls how Mary sometimes complains about his what she calls *anal retentiveness*. Creases in trousers, no crumbs anywhere, that sort of thing. Rachel isn't certain, but she thinks punctuality is a concern of his too.

Dan has somehow taken the bottle of wine from her without Rachel noticing. Her arms are still folded into a cradle, but they are empty. She lets them fall stiffly to her side as they enter the formal living room. There he is: her date. She hadn't expected him to have a goatee. Rachel does not like facial hair. And she'd imagined him to be taller, like Dan. Weren't they cousins?

"We're having Mount Gay and tonics," Dan says, handing her one.

Rachel takes it, but frowns. They don't seem to go together—rum with tonic. She'd rather have gin and tonic. It occurs to her that she might not like Dan. There is music playing, Emmylou Harris, she thinks. Or one of those women that Peter used to call depressed female singers.

"Where's Mary?" Rachel asks. The drink actually doesn't taste too bad. She tries to relax.

"Working some culinary wonder, as usual," Dan says.

Rachel looks at the cousin. "So you're an architect, Mary tells me?"

"I *studied* architecture," he says. He is glum. Probably over the girlfriend. Rachel is certain he was dumped; he has that look about him.

"It's fascinating really," Dan says. "Harry is restoring some buildings in Paris. They were going to be torn down and he's rescued them, haven't you?"

"You live in Paris?" Rachel asks, almost angry. What a waste of time. A date with a man who lives an entire ocean away.

"Part of the time," Harry says. "I keep a flat there."

Rachel finds it pretentious when Americans call apartments flats. She finishes her drink and plays with the ice cubes, letting them knock against each other and clink against the sides of the glass. The glass has a bridge etched on it.

"We refill without too much commotion here." It's Harry who speaks, laughing and standing right in front of her. "A simple, 'May I have another' usually does the trick."

Rachel blushes. "Well then," she says, handing him her empty glass. Up close, he's actually kind of sexy. This surprises her. Not tall, no, but built well. And she likes his shirt. She hadn't noticed it when she'd come in, but it's a vintage 1950s Hawaiian shirt, in really awful colors, orange and green and mustard yellow.

Mary comes in then, all fluttery and silly, with a plate of cheese and crackers.

"How's it going in here?" she asks, looking in Rachel's direction.

Harry hands Rachel a fresh drink.

"I see you've got a drink," Mary says, happily.

They all sit back down and Mary tells the same details about Harry's work in Paris.

"Where are these buildings you're saving?" Rachel asks. The rum has made her bold.

"The fifteenth arrondisement," Harry says.

"Near that big cemetery? The one with Chopin and Gertrude Stein and everyone?" Rachel asks him.

"Yes," he answers, obviously excited. "You know Paris?"

"Well, I spent time there, years ago. Almost ten years ago, I guess. I was there in winter. And it rained all the time. That made it even more perfect, roaming around that cemetery in the cold rain."

"Yes," Harry says. "It would."

"We rented a drafty apartment near Notre Dame." Rachel tries to keep her voice from catching. But a rush of warm memories slide over her. The peeling paint on the walls, the sourish smell of falafels from a stand below, the lumpy mattress on their bed. She can almost hear Peter's poor attempts at romancing her in French. *Shut the door, shut the door,* he whispered each night as he moved inside her, and Rachel would struggle for a way to do that, to somehow close their bedroom door— though it only opened into a high ceilinged sitting room filled with faded velvet high backed chairs and a worn sofa whose stuffing fell out and floated around the apartment like the fluff from old dandelions. It was weeks before she realized what Peter was whispering to her: *Je t'adore.*

Harry has rested his hand lightly on her bare arm.

"You have fond memories of living in Paris," he says.

Rachel can manage only a nod.

"Maybe someday you'll go back?" he asks.

"Yes," she tells him, surprising herself with the enthusiasm in her voice, as if by going back she could reclaim something.

THEN LATER, AT DINNER—Mary has made sate, shrimp and chicken, with jasmine rice—Rachel and Harry have their heads bent together like old friends. She is telling him about Europe, how she and Peter spent two years there. She doesn't mention Peter by name, or that she later married him. Instead, she calls him *my friend*; she says *we*.

"We managed to get into Eastern Europe. That was something," she says.

"Ten years ago?" Harry whistles. "I wish I'd seen it back then."

"I had no idea you were such an adventurer," Mary says. "Hitchhiking around Europe and such."

"Mary knows me better as the crazed mother making sure my daughter doesn't fall head first off the curly slide," Rachel explains.

"You have a daughter?" Harry asks her.

"She has a Sophia!" Mary tells him.

"Spelled differently," Dan adds.

"Mine is S-O-F-I-A," Rachel begins.

Harry finishes for her. "Like the city," he says.

WHEN HARRY HEARS where she lives, he insists on driving her home. "You can't walk there at this time of night," he tells her.

It is very late. After dinner, they all go outside and eat strawberry shortcake on the patio. Dan brings out a bottle of grappa that he and Mary got in Italy.

"Is that when you saw the pope?" Harry asks. It is obvious this is a joke between them.

"Yes," Dan says, "that's when we saw the pope."

By the time they are leaving, Rachel feels happy. She lets Harry take her arm. She agrees to his offer of a ride home. His car is a beat up Triumph Spitfire with a noisy muffler. She tries to ask something once, but the muffler is too loud. They cannot talk. When they get to her house, and he turns off the car, the silence almost hurts her ears. She thinks of how after rock concerts her ears would feel this way when she walked outside. This is something Harry would appreciate, but when she turns to tell him he has already moved out of the car and is opening her door for her.

"I would like to come in," he tells her.

It is odd, but since that first rush of memories about Paris, Rachel cannot get the idea of it out of her mind. She misses Peter, yes. But she misses more than just him. She wants *that* again. The kind of love they had then, in Paris, and all the rest of their time in Europe, the months in Krakow and Sofia, the nights spent sleeping tangled together in second class compartments on trains, speeding toward—toward what? A future, she supposed. A future that was good, and right. She did not think of any of that then, drinking bad Polish coffee in the early morning, or walking the gray streets of Sofia, each tucking a hand into the other's coat pocket, or chewing the yeasty warm rolls that every Hungarian bakery seemed to sell. You don't think of the *rightness* of things then; you simply bask in it. Later, when you find yourself on a sidewalk in Providence late at night with a stranger, it all comes back—why, Rachel can almost *taste* those rolls! She takes Harry's hand. It is small for a man's hand, and soft. She takes it in hers and leads him inside.

MARY CALLS, FIRST thing Sunday morning. She has just come back from church—She goes to church? Rachel thinks, blinking against the sun that filters in between the slats of her mini-blinds—and, Mary squeaks into the phone, she only has a minute but she really really thinks that Harry liked Rachel. Rachel stifles a laugh. She is finding out that Mary is oddly innocent.

"I'm sure he'll call you," Mary is saying.

She sounds almost schoolgirlish, and for a moment

Rachel imagines her in the plaid skirt and cardigan uniform of some Catholic church.

"I think he will," Rachel manages. A conversation with a *real* friend would play so differently. She knows this. She can still smell Harry on her sheets; her thighs are sticky from him.

"All of that stuff about Europe," Mary says. "He ate that up."

Rachel stifles more laughter. She promises to tell Mary every detail when he does call. She promises to get the girls together later in the week. Until finally she can hang up, and go back to sleep.

WHEN HE FINALLY does call, on Wednesday, she invites him over for lunch. It is her day off, and Rachel is reworking her résumé. She does not want to manage the toy store anymore. In fact, she is sick of managing things. Rachel puts all of the papers aside, into a heap, on the kitchen table, and makes poached chicken. Then she pours herself a glass of wine—So decadent, she thinks, drinking wine in the middle of the day—and waits.

Harry arrives late, breathless. She is struck again by how small he is, and how she has spent so much time with large men. Perhaps, she decides, as he forgoes the poached chicken and instead undresses her right there in the kitchen, perhaps she has wasted her time on large men. Here she is, making love on her kitchen table—she sits, he stands, and they are eye to eye. Her résumé flutters to the floor. Like snow, she thinks. Like fallout. Like the stuffing from that old sofa in Paris. Is it an omen? She tries to focus on what she is doing, her legs wrapped around Harry's waist, her breath coming out in tight little gasps, but she is too far ahead of herself, past this moment and seeing somewhere down the road. Living near that cemetery in Paris, Sofia in a Madeline outfit—blue coat, yellow hat, and Harry taking her like this, on tables and in doorways. What a future, she sees as Harry collapses against her, done.

Rachel puts her hands on the back of his neck. She can feel the bristly hair growing there. The tops of his ears are red.

"We've made quite a mess," he says, looking down at her papers.

He bends to pick them up, and she is suddenly embarrassed at what she had been thinking just a moment before. This man is a stranger. His body, in daylight, reminds her of a rooster, compact and sure of itself. He struts, she realizes as he gathers all of her papers and hands them to her. He has freckles she did not know about, an appendectomy scar.

"My résumé," she says, for something to say. The air between them has gotten to that fragile place.

He brightens. "That's why I called," he says.

She wishes he would put on his pants, but he doesn't. Rooster, she thinks again, and pulls her tee shirt over her head.

"All of our talk the other night, about Europe, and how you'd like to go back. The office I work with there needs someone. It's a one year thing, a funny job really. Kind of a goodwill person, to woo possible donors for the restoration project. You would take them to the various sites, take them to dinner, the Louvre and the Eiffel Tower."

"My French isn't great," she says, stopping him. It's too much, what he's telling her.

"That's the thing. They want an American. Most of these donors are British or American."

"Really?" she says. She has stepped too far forward and too far back. Rachel tries to return to somewhere in the middle. Aren't all people strangers when they first meet? she thinks. She tries to remember Peter as a stranger. Once he was someone she did not yet know.

Harry has moved closer to her. "Are you interested?" he asks.

"Definitely," Rachel says.

SHE DUTIFULLY REPORTS the phone call and the lunch at her house—he did stay and eat the poached chicken and finish the bottle of wine with her—to Mary at the playground on Thursday. Of course, Rachel leaves out what happened on the kitchen tab le, and the job possibility.

"He seems really enthusiastic," Rachel says as a finale to their date.

But Mary is frowning.

Rachel sighs. She thought Mary wanted something to happen between her and Harry. Once again she is reminded of how little she knows about Mary—who she really is, what she expects.

"Did he ask you out again?" Mary says. Now she is watching the girls come down the bright orange curly slide.

"Not in so many words," Rachel says. She tries a different approach. "I like him. He's not my usual type and I think that's good."

"Mmmmm," Mary says. She has started to nibble on dried fruit. For extra vitamins during her pregnancy, she explained earlier.

"My ex-husband is very big. Tall and burly," Rachel continues, though she wants to stop. Mary is annoying her. "I kind of like Harry's size. And he's very funny."

"If he hasn't actually *said* he'll call again, maybe he won't," Mary says.

"Thanks a lot," Rachel blurts. Mary was probably a virgin when she got married, she thinks. She doesn't *know* anything. Still, she has managed to make Rachel feel unsettled.

In the distance, Sofia pauses at the top of the slide to wave. "Watch me, Mommy," she calls. "Are you watching?"

Rachel thinks of this often as the days pass and Harry doesn't call. Maybe Mary had known something, after all. Maybe she even knew about the kitchen table. Or the job. She would be upset that Rachel hadn't told her everything. So would she then keep some information from Rachel? Throughout the weekend—it rains every day—as she thinks of ways to occupy Sofia, she almost calls Mary several times. She almost calls Harry. But in the end she just helps Sofia make a large floor puzzle of Madeline and Pepito, watches *Mary Poppins* and *The Wizard of Oz* too many times, and eats a lot of junk food. By the time Monday comes, Rachel is relieved to see Sofia off to day care, relieved even to go to work at the toy store.

RACHEL HAS COME up with a list of excuses. He knows that Sofia is away this coming weekend; he will ask her out for Friday night. He is waiting the obligatory week between dates. He is in Paris. He is dead.

She goes to the interview in Boston on Wednesday,

dressed in her most sophisticated suit and a pair of borrowed patent leather Mary Janes with chunky heels that her friend Liz swears are "in." Although she does not expect to see Harry, she decides that if she does, he will see how great she can look.

In fact, she doesn't see him. Instead, she sails from office to office in Government Center, talking to different people who are delighted to see her—*Harry says you're perfect for this job!*—and who, finally, simply, offer her the job. She can start in September. She will have to move to Paris. They have lists of apartments, of schools for Sofia, of shipping companies for her furniture; they give her maps and a guide to Paris and a little booklet called *Now that You Are an American Living in Paris.* They say, *Harry was right! You're perfect for this job.*

Still, no word from Harry.

But Rachel feels her life has taken a right turn, after three years of wrong moves and bad decisions. She looks around her crummy apartment and imagines where she and Sofia will be in two short months. Fuck Harry, she thinks. And when she explains to Sofia about the job, her daughter's eyes grow wide. "Will I meet Madeline?" she says. "And Miss Clavel?" Rachel, for an instant, almost thinks they might.

THE FIRST THING that goes wrong is that Rachel forgets to pack Sofia's Madeline doll for her weekend with Peter.

"I'm not even going to discuss her overdependence on her T-O—" Peter barks into the telephone.

"T-O?" Rachel asks him. She is already edgy. They are in

the middle of a huge thunderstorm and she hates talking on the phone during storms.

"Transitional object," Peter explains. Rachel is sure this is something Yvonne says. "The point right now," he continues, "is that she's hysterical and I can't change her overdependence in one night, so you have to bring it over right now."

Lightning scars the sky.

"Drive all the way down there? In this?" Rachel says. It's a half hour in good weather. There are curvy roads, traffic.

She can hear Sofia crying in the background.

"I'm on my way," she tells Peter.

But before she can leave the phone rings again. Maybe he has calmed her down, Rachel thinks, and answers it.

"Rachel? It's Mary." She sounds nervous. "I have to tell you something."

"This isn't a good time," Rachel says. "Sofia is with her father and she's upset—"

"Harry is back with Victoria. There. I've said it. Ever since that day at the playground I've been feeling just awful, because I knew they were back—they got back together the very next night after you met him—"

"The next night?" Rachel asks, to be certain she is hearing correctly. She sits down, holding Madeline on her lap. "That's impossible."

"Maybe he saw you for lunch just to be polite, to be friends, you know," Mary is saying.

Rachel thinks about him strutting naked around her kitchen. "I don't think so," she tells Mary. *That's why I called,* he had said. About the job. She thinks of her poached chicken, the open bottle of wine, and feels embarrassed.

"Look," Mary says, her voice easier now, "the point is I wanted you to know. It's crazy really. They're actually getting married. Can you believe it? All in a matter of days. It's crazy."

"I think Dan's cousin is a shit," Rachel says. "A real shit. Trust me, he did not come over here for cookies and milk and a round of 'Kumbaya.'"

Rachel hears Mary's sharp intake of breath. "I'm certain I don't know," Mary says.

"Well, I do. All he wanted was . . ." She struggles a moment, then says, "All he wanted was a good piece of ass. I'm sure he's very happy, the little rooster."

She knows she has shocked Mary and for some reason, she's glad.

"I know you've got to go," Mary says, sounding too composed. "I won't keep you."

After they hang up, Rachel realizes it is the first time they have ever spoken without planning a play date.

BY THE TIME she gets to Peter's the storm is over and Sofia is asleep. Rachel stands on the doorstep of the home he shares with another woman, holding the doll out to him. When she told him about Paris, assuring him it was just one year and that Sofia could spend a chunk of that time with him, he had been happy for her. *I knew you'd make your way,* he'd told her.

Now he is looking at her funny.

"What?" Rachel says.

Peter shakes his head. "You look so pretty," he says.

"That's all." When she doesn't say anything he opens the door wider and asks her inside. He tells her Yvonne is teaching a class at the Y on grooming cats.

Rachel tries not to study everything in the house. She sees that animal hair coats everything. She sees framed photographs of Peter and Yvonne, all smiling white teeth. She smells some kind of fruity candle burning, one of those cloyingly sweet ones that make her slightly nauseous. But she concentrates on Peter's back, the back she has followed through train stations across Europe, and up narrow stairways in pensions, and into crowds, and now through the house he shares with Yvonne. When he turns to ask her if she'd like a glass of wine, she is startled by him, by how she has loved him for so long. She actually gasps, she thinks. But he is too busy, uncorking and pouring, to notice.

She lets herself look around this room. Here is their television, their stereo, a rough Haitian rug that used to sit in the apartment Rachel lived in with Peter. Music is playing, something unfamiliar. A CD case lying on the floor says ENYA, but Rachel doesn't know if that's the group or the title.

"To Paris," Peter says, raising his glass.

"Shut the door," Rachel says. But she is thinking *je t'adore.*

She lets him kiss her. But she does the rest, the undressing, the reaching, the urging *yes, yes, yes.* For a few minutes they are somewhere else, on some forgotten bed in a foreign country, doing this same thing, learning each other. But when this is done, she feels something she has not yet felt about Peter: *it is over between them.* The thought strikes her, like a slap. Then settles into its proper place. It really is over, she thinks. When they hear Yvonne's car pull up, they both scramble to their feet and dress hurriedly, without embarrassment.

For the first time, when Rachel sees Yvonne, she smiles.

"I was on my way out," she tells her.

"We had a minor tragedy," Peter says.

RACHEL GIVES HER notice at the toy store and spends her days with Sofia at the playground, or at home packing. Her friends have started to give her going away parties. She feels full, happy even. Later, when she sits alone in her small bathroom, two weeks before she and Sofia are to leave, staring at the bright pink spot appearing in front of her—*a pink spot is positive!*—Rachel wonders if she ignored the early signs just to have those weeks of feeling so good. Her hands are shaking as she lowers the early pregnancy test with its positive pink reading. She wants to call Mary suddenly, Mary who she has not spoken to since that awful phone call. And as soon as she thinks about doing it, she understands why—this could have something to do with Harry.

THERE IS ONLY one right thing to do. Rachel knows this. But still she calls her friend Liz—a *real* friend—and tells her. Liz is single, self-assured, a lawyer who wears suits in bright colors like magenta and tangerine.

"It could be Peter's?" Liz asks.

It is the one question that Rachel has not let herself consider. Because there, in front of her every moment, singing

"Frère Jacques" and skipping through the emptying rooms and splashing in her bath each night, is Sofia, the child she did have. Hers and Peter's child.

"It could be that rooster's too," Rachel says, too quickly.

Liz recovers immediately. "That's irrelevant anyway," she says, in what Rachel guesses is her lawyer voice. "Let's not waste time. Call your doctor. Set up an appointment." Then, gentler, "You only have two weeks before you go."

"I know," Rachel says.

Outside, Sofia's voice rises up to her through the open windows. It is late summer, the air has not yet turned cool. Everything around them has gone past green to gold and looks burned, parched. A wave of nausea washes over Rachel. Is it her first? She remembers thinking she had food poisoning at a picnic last week. She remembers thinking she might be coming down with something.

"I'll drive you," Liz says. "Let me check my calendar."

"No," Rachel tells her. She is thinking of other things. That flight to Paris in two weeks. The way a plane points straight upward when it's first airborne.

"Look," Liz tells her, "you're not alone here."

Rachel knows this. She has Sofia, after all.

She cannot find a doctor to do it.

"My God," she tells Liz the night before, "it's like the sixties or something. I mean, this is legal, right?"

In the end, there is no place to go except a clinic, where everyone else will be twenty years younger than her, clutching the hand of a frightened boy or a disappointed mother.

Rachel almost asks Mary to watch Sofia for the day. She has been asking, *Won't I even get to say goodbye to Sophia?* and Rachel has made up ridiculous stories about why they haven't played together. Now, after all this time of not calling, she cannot bring herself to finally do it to ask for a favor. She believes that Mary is sitting in her lovely cool home, expecting that Rachel *will* eventually call. But somehow that is even worse, the idea that she would call and Mary would gush, forgive, go back.

So she leaves Sofia with Peter and Yvonne, who acts troubled by the surprise midweek intrusion. *Sofia will have to stay with us at the office,* they say like a threat. *We have appointments to keep.* Rachel knows those appointments, the rabies shots and neutering and hairball removals. But Sofia likes that idea. She will help with the animals. She will make them better. Oddly, in these weeks before they leave for Paris, she has neglected her Madeline doll. She leaves it now, as she runs to her father, tossed in a corner like an orphan.

Rachel has decided to walk to the clinic; she is too nervous, pent-up is how she thinks of it, to ride in a car and circle around for a parking space. Liz will pick her up at two. She has opted for anesthesia and she will, they advised her, be groggy, too groggy to drive or walk alone.

The heat of the day makes her stomach flip-flop. And, walking, she is aware of her breasts, the fullness there. She is definitely pregnant. *Why now?* she wonders, when everything was finally going so right. But then she stops herself from that line of thinking. She has managed, hasn't she? She has packed up her and Sofia's lives, she has—long distance!—found them a new place to live. At night she listens to language tapes, carefully repeating the phrases. *Comment ça va? Je m'appelle Rachel. Ou est la gare du nord?*

And she has managed this. This phone calls. The hushed voices. The appointment. On the phone the receptionist had warned her that Thursday was known with pro-life groups as baby killing day. Rachel supposed that was a test, a way of asking if she had the guts to actually go through with it, if she was certain she was doing the right thing.

Now, though, as she turns the corner onto the street where the clinic sits, she realizes that the receptionist has given her a real warning. In the wavery heat, the clinic practically shimmers. Rachel thinks of Oz, and then of those religious sightings people have—the madonna in clouds, in tortillas, in tree bark. She thinks of those because when shown on television, some camera desperately attempting to catch a glimpse of the image, there is always a crowd, shouting. Praying, Rachel supposed. Here, in front of the clinic, is a crowd too. A shouting crowd, carrying signs.

A knife of fear stabs Rachel in the gut. It is wrong, she thinks, that she should have to walk through them to go inside. She watches a teenage girl get swallowed up by them.

"Baby killer," they shout.

"What about the Commandments?" someone calls. "Thou shall not kill."

Rachel waits, but she never sees the girl emerge. It is as if they really have swallowed her up.

She is not sure what propels her forward, closer, until she is right upon them. A van parked nearby says CATHOLICS FOR BABIES RIGHTS on the side. Rachel too was a Catholic, was raised that way. She thinks of the cathedrals in Europe, the darkness of them, the heavy smell of incense, the way your footsteps echoed as you made your way forward.

"Baby killer!" they are shouting. At her, she realizes.

She is overwhelmed by the idea of her daughter, of Sofia. The softness of her skin and the brown sugary smell she carries with her. But even more than that. All the things that make her Sofia. The scramble of cells and genes. Everything.

Rachel makes her way almost through the crowd, almost to the door, when she is stopped by something so familiar she smiles and reaches out to it. But her arm hangs like that, reaching, without going any farther. It is Mary that she sees. In that crowd, wielding a sign that does not hide her bulging belly, which is wrapped in the softest color yellow maternity dress. Mary sees her too. Their eyes meet, lock. It seems to Rachel that the world around them melts completely away, and they are just two women standing on a street. But then the clinic door opens, releasing a medicinal smell in its burst of cold air-conditioned air, and two people emerge and gently take Rachel's arms to escort her safely inside. Behind her, the shouting starts up again, and Rachel almost imagines that she hears Mary's voice above all the others, calling out to her. But when the door closes, and she is in the silent waiting room, she cannot imagine what it might be that Mary would have to say to her. Or what she could ever say to Mary.

THE LANGUAGE

OF SORROW

———————————

THE BUS FROM Logan Airport pulled in with a heavy sigh. Dora's grandson was coming from New York City, via Kennedy Airport. Gate one. She considered getting a box of doughnuts to bring home with them. A Dunkin' Donuts was right inside the terminal, Dora had recognized the familiar smell before she even saw the shop. Her children had always loved doughnuts, especially the messy ones like powdered sugar or chocolate frosted. A long ago morning shot through Dora's mind: Tillie and Dan at the old metal kitchen table, the one with the green rooster on top, their mouths dusted with white sugar, with smears of chocolate, their teeth small and smooth, the sunlight sending dust particles dancing in the air, and Dora pouring purple Kool-Aid from a pitcher with a goofy grinning face on the front.

She remembered it and it was gone. As if she could somehow pull it back, Dora raised her hand, surprising herself. The hand looked like her grandmother's used to—wrinkled, spotted, gnarly. The noisy arrival of a bus right in front of her forced Dora to put all of this nonsense aside. It was the bus from New York City. On that bus was her own grandson, Dan's boy, who she had not seen in over five years. People spilled off the bus. Giggling girls and boys who looked like they were in gangs, young women with small children and older women dressed in clothes from Lord and Taylor or somewhere like that. Dora met each person's gaze with her own expectant one. Her lipstick felt waxy on her lips. Fleetingly she remembered how the undertaker had put a thick coat of lipstick on her friend Madeline Dumfey's lips, in a dreadful shade of pink. He thought it made her look healthy, as if someone who'd been killed by cancer could look healthy. What an idiot, Dora thought. The flow of people slowed, then stopped. Dora stood on tiptoes, trying to see inside the bus. Was it the wrong day? The wrong bus?

But then a boy stepped off. He was not like the tattooed and pierced teenagers who Dora saw on Thayer Street. This disappointed her for reasons she did not quite understand. He was more like the private school boys, the ones who dragged lacrosse sticks past her house every afternoon. Except for the dark shadows beneath his eyes and the defeated way in which he slouched off the bus, he could be one of them. Sad and ordinary, those were the words that sprang to Dora's mind. His hands clutched a piece of bright red American Tourister luggage, the one meant for women to carry their curlers and things. With his fair hair and pale skin, his light blue eyes and perfect pouty lips, he looked exactly like his mother. This disappointed Dora too.

"Peter," she said, stepping through the crowd waiting for their luggage.

He barely looked at her. "I've got another bag," he said, and joined the others waiting.

"Let's get it, shall we?" she said, though he had already gone to do just that.

The last time she had seen him was five years ago at her son's funeral, a hot bright sunlit day, even though it was February. That was Houston, she supposed. Relentlessly sunny, even in winter, even at funerals. She had not paid much attention to Peter that day. She'd had enough to deal with. The news of Dan's death and the way in which he'd died. The flight to Texas in the middle of the night, stopping and changing planes in Newark and then Chicago and then Dallas. Arriving just in time to get to the church, unable to even change her clothes. Peter seemed hardly there that day.

"I've got it," he said.

Dora blinked as if he woke her up.

"Welcome to Providence," she said, hoping he didn't notice her voice trembling.

His eyes looked like some kind of monster's eyes they were such a light blue. Dora found herself remembering a little albino girl who'd gone to school with Tillie.

"I don't want to be here," Peter said. He swung his other bag, also bright red, the kind men hung their suits in, over his shoulder. The weight of it made him stagger slightly.

Before Dora could think what to say, he was walking ahead of her, his shadow stretching between them like a bridge.

SHE PUT HIM in Tillie's old room. It still had the pink and white striped wallpaper from her childhood, and a bureau decorated with ballerinas. Even though he frowned when he saw it Dora couldn't let him stay in Dan's room. He didn't seem to deserve it, the smell of boy things, the stamps and coins carefully collected or the models of ships and race cars assembled over many lost Saturday afternoons. This boy seemed removed from any of that, a sullen stranger plunked into Dora's life.

Peter tossed his bags on the bed. "Thanks," he said. Dora heard sarcasm in that one simple word.

"I could get us some doughnuts," she said without much conviction. "We could have some doughnuts and chat a little."

He wasn't even looking at her. His eyes flitted around the room, searching. "Is there a phone I could use?"

Dora hesitated. His mother had told her he wasn't supposed to call the girl.

"There's one in the kitchen," Dora said carefully. "And one in my room. But I'm afraid you can't call . . ." What was the girl's name?

"Rebecca," Peter said. "But I have to." He walked right past Dora and pointed foolishly like the scarecrow in *The Wizard of Oz.* "Which way to the kitchen?"

Dora put her hand on his arm. Startled, she dropped it just as quickly. She didn't expect muscles under the shirt. And standing close like this she saw that he was taller than he'd seemed at the bus station.

"Your mother gave me so few restrictions. Calling Rebecca is one of them. I'm sorry."

He looked at her and she knew that really, she couldn't stop him.

"You love her, I suppose," she said.

He laughed, a barking sound that Dora didn't like one

bit. "No. But I don't think I should have deserted her. I don't think I should have been sent away for the entire summer to live in this podunk town with an old lady."

Dora took a step back, away from him, rubbing her arms up and down.

"I mean," Peter said, "who are you, you know? My father kills himself and you vanish. Do you know what I've been going through for five whole years? You have no idea."

She did know, of course; Melinda had filled her in. But what Dora said was, "I hardly think your father killed himself."

That bark again, then Peter stuck his face in hers. "What do you call it when someone smokes so much cocaine that they jump out a fifth-story window running from imaginary monsters? Huh?"

Dora reared up to her full height, five feet, eight inches. She had always believed in the benefit of calcium and as a result had not shrunk like other women her age. Why, Madeline Dumfey had died a full three inches shorter than she had lived.

"An accident," Dora said, "I call it an accident."

DORA DID NOT see the point of dwelling on her losses. But often, at night, they seized her and shook her awake. Sometimes she found herself groping for Bill on the other side of the bed, reaching and reaching as if her life depended on finding him there until, finally, panting, she had to remind herself that he had died on April 14, 1983, from lung cancer. A picture of him taking those last gasping breaths in a hospital bed would come to her and she would close her eyes and press the lids hard until it vanished.

Other times she awoke thinking she had to call Madeline about one thing or another and then a strange uneasiness took hold as Dora remembered that Madeline was dead. They had known each other since 1943 when they worked side by side as secretaries at the army base in Quonset Point. Dora wore her hair in a Veronica Lake peekaboo cut back then; Madeline favored more of a Gene Tierney wave. They went together every Friday afternoon after work to Isabella's Parisian Hair Salon in Wickford to get their hair done. Both of them had slim hips, good legs, a wide collection of shoes. They shared nylons, a real commodity back then, and lipstick. They double-dated, covered for each other when they wanted to give a guy the bum's rush. They stood up for each other at their weddings; Dora wore a deep maroon velvet for Madeline's and Madeline wore an icy blue satin at Dora's. Those were the things that came to mind when Dora woke up with an urgency to call Madeline: the smell of the chemicals at their beauty parlor near the base, the feel of a nylon stocking sliding on her leg, the crush of velvet against cool skin on a November morning.

Since Peter had arrived, what woke Dora was the feeling that she needed to check on the children, the way she would when they were young. She used to walk through the darkness of the house and slip into their rooms and make sure they were breathing. First Tillie, a neat sleeper, on her back with her covers tucked under her chin. Then Dan, often upside down in his bed, his sheets and blankets a tangle around his waist and feet. Dora would stand and count their breaths before climbing back into her own bed, satisfied.

PETER SAT IN the kitchen, ate entire boxes of Oreo cookies, drank milk straight from the bottle, and talked to Rebecca. At first Dora reprimanded him, reminding him of her promise to his mother. But Peter would just stare at her with those practically albino eyes, popping whole cookies into his mouth while she explained. Really, Dora didn't care if he talked to the girl. Talking wasn't going to change anything. So she gave up and let him do it.

". . . so Polly's coming over a lot? Her mother lets her?" Dora heard him say one afternoon.

Dora was making baked scrod for dinner, with parsley potatoes. He didn't like anything she cooked but she continued to make complete meals for the two of them despite that. Over her roast beef and mashed potatoes he'd asked her if there was anyplace around to get a good burrito. The night she'd made leg of lamb he'd requested fish sticks. Last night he'd described something called Hot Pockets, a frozen bread type thing stuffed with meat and vegetables. Dora had nodded and taken another pork chop from the platter.

"I'm surprised her mother lets her. Really surprised. Her mother's like so uptight. She's a Republican, you know."

Dora glanced at him. *She* was a Republican, after all. But she would have let Tillie visit her pregnant friend. She would have considered it a positive experience for Tillie, to know that there were consequences for actions.

"What?" Peter said, cupping his hand over the mouthpiece of the phone.

Dora spread the crumbled Ritz crackers over the scrod

and put the pan in the oven. "I think you have foolish ideas, that's all," she said, and set the timer.

"Excuse me," Peter said. "But I wasn't talking to you."

Dora shrugged.

"You're eavesdropping," he said.

"I'm making dinner," Dora told him.

"Anyway, I think Polly is probably sick of Jen and Justin and that's why she's hanging around so much," Peter said, presumably not to Dora.

Dora took out two of the blue and white everyday dishes and began to set the table around Peter. She tried to picture the girl on the other end, but could only come up with an image of Melinda at that age, a sullen girl who always looked like she was not to be trusted. She'd slunk into their home during dinner one night, Dan's arm protectively around her waist, dressed in torn jeans and brown suede Indian moccasins. Those shoes had bothered Dora. Earlier that day she had commented to Madeline Dumfey that it seemed loose girls wore those. Then right in her kitchen, hanging on to her son, Melinda appeared with that very type of shoe. "That girl's trouble," Dora had announced as soon as Melinda and Dan had gone. And of course she'd been right. Before Melinda he had never even gotten drunk. After Melinda's appearance in their kitchen Dan had started with marijuana and who knew what else. The school was calling every other day about his absences. One night the police brought him home, stoned, confused, and with Melinda.

Dora sighed. She was holding two forks, the timer was buzzing, and Peter was staring at her hard.

"Gran?" he said.

She shook her head. "I'm fine." She went to the oven for

the scrod, her heart twisted in grief. In her own lifetime she had taken chances. When she was only twenty she'd fallen foolishly in love with a married man. He had taken her to a lopsided ski cabin he and his wife owned in Maine and Dora lost her virginity on the floor there; he felt too guilty to have sex in his marriage bed. The next morning, feeling reckless, Dora took two runs down the bunny slope, then boarded the chairlift to the top of the mountain where she promptly fell and broke her leg. The man drove her home in a stony silence and never called her again. My how she had carried on! she remembered now, making Madeline drive her past his house, her leg stuck in that awful cast for two entire months, a reminder of her indiscretion.

She'd told servicemen on their way overseas that she loved them when she didn't, sad young men who did not always come back. Dora had enjoyed the way they used to cling to her, as if she mattered more than anything else. She remembered one young man from Pennsylvania who was headed to France. He had cried after they'd made love because he was so afraid to die. So she knew about risk, how any of those trysts could have resulted in pregnancy, how the wife could have discovered the affair. And worse. When her own children were small she'd had an affair with Bill's partner, an affair that lasted almost two years. She'd even considered leaving Bill for him. Talk about risk. There were dinners with the man and his wife, even a week long vacation together in Puerto Rico with all of their children. Like the foolish people they were, Dora and the man had met every night on the beach and made love while Bill and Gloria looked over them from the twenty-eighth floor of the Old San Juan Hotel.

But all of that was nothing compared to Dan. Dora liked

to blame Melinda for what happened but she knew the truth: it was drugs that took her son from her. He and Melinda drifted around a world that Dora could not even imagine. They moved from job to job and city to city so much that entire months passed when she couldn't even find them. Landlords had no forwarding address, operators had no new numbers. Finally the night came when Dan called Dora, waking her from a fitful sleep. He was leaving Melinda, he'd told her. He was checking into rehab. "I have to save myself," he'd said, and she heard the desperateness in his voice. Dora still could feel the way dryness gripped her throat that night. She'd hung up and drunk glass after glass of water, unable to quench the horrible thirst. Before she hung up she'd told him that she would pay for treatment, if that's what it took. She told him it was about time he'd realized where Melinda had led him. "If you leave her," she'd said, "you can come back here and start over. You can even bring the boy." It wasn't until a week later, when she got the call that he was dead, that Dora regretted all she hadn't said that night. She hadn't said she was proud of him for finally realizing he needed help. She hadn't told him she loved him.

"Gran!" Peter shouted, and he ran over to her.

That was when Dora felt the hot butter on her leg, burning her as it dripped from the pan. She let the boy take the fish from her and lead her to a chair. Already an ugly blister appeared on her calf, and smaller ones ran down to her ankle like a trail of tears.

"I'm all right," she said.

But she stayed seated, feeling the hot pain surge through her as Peter grabbed a dishtowel and ice cubes. She watched him move through the kitchen as if she were watching a movie. His own strong calves under khaki shorts, the golden hair on his arms. A stranger, kneeling at her feet, pressing a cool cloth to her burns.

"Thank you," she said.

He nodded.

Dora took her hand and placed it on his bent head. She kept it there until he looked up, searching for a clue that she was fine. The thing was, Dora did not want him to go away from her. She didn't want to let go.

"Another minute," she lied. "Just another minute." Again Dora rested her hand on his head.

CHECK THE CHILDREN. Stumbling, Dora pulled on her robe and walked barefoot down the dark hallway. She should get a nightlight, she thought as she pushed open the door to Tillie's room. A nightlight to keep everyone safe. Tillie's bed was a mess, the summer quilt in the tumbling blocks pattern was on the floor, the sheets a knot beside it. Not at all like Tillie, Dora thought, her heart racing. She took another step into the room before she remembered. Tillie was in California. That's where she lived. Dan's boy slept here now.

Her heart still beating fast, Dora dropped onto the chair at Tillie's old desk, where photographs of Tillie as a teenager stared back at her. She had taken ballet forever, then without warning switched to modern dance. Even though Dora never really enjoyed those later performances, she'd enjoyed watching her daughter. In one of the pictures, Tillie sat on the grass at Roger Williams Park, strumming a guitar, grinning. Braless, the outline of her nipples poked through the cotton tee shirt. Dora lifted the picture to look closer.

Right after Dan had died, that very next winter, Tillie had a breast cancer scare. They'd done a lumpectomy, some radiation. Dora had flown out to San Francisco to be with her, had driven her through the maze of unfamiliar streets to doctors and hospitals, keeping her tone upbeat even as her gut ached with fear. When Madeline Dumfey drove Dora to Logan Airport for her flight to San Francisco, she asked her if she felt life was being unfair to her. Bill gone. And Dan. And now Tillie sick. Dora had been surprised by the question. Life unfair? She had known three big loves, she had borne two children, she had traveled as far as China, she was old and alive, she had her own health. She had listed these things to Madeline. "But to lose everyone," Madeline had said. "Really, Dora, you must let yourself get angry. You must." Someone, Dora no longer remembered who, had once said that one death was a tragedy, but many deaths were a statistic. Dora told Madeline this and Madeline had blinked back at her in that way she had, part disbelief, part disgust. "Really, Dora. That's a terrible thing to say."

Now here was Madeline, dead, and Tillie fine except for a small ugly scar on her left breast. Dora did not feel equipped to understand any of it. What of all those boys she'd held who'd been killed in the Pacific, at Omaha Beach, at sea? What of the other men she'd loved, dead now too, both of them? Bill's partner had died right at the Museum of Fine Arts in Boston, in front of a Winslow Homer painting, of a massive heart attack. If that hadn't happened, it was possible that she would have run off with him.

Standing, Dora heard the low hum of a voice downstairs.

She followed it, carefully holding the banister as she walked. There in the kitchen, hanging up the telephone, was Peter. He looked at her, weary.

"It could be any day now," he said. "She's dilated two centimeters. Her back hurts."

Dora allowed herself to ask the question that had been on her lips since Melinda had first called back in the spring.

"Why the hell didn't she get an abortion?" Dora said.

"She's Baptist. You know. Super religious. She thinks she'll go to hell for something like that."

"That's plain stupid," Dora said. She sat across from Peter. "What kind of nincompoop is this girl?"

He laughed. For the first time it did not sound like a harsh bark. Dora laughed too.

SHE TOOK HIM to lunch at the Rue de L'Espoir. "You can't sit waiting by the phone," she told him as she hustled him into the car. "Having a baby can take a very long time. I was in labor twenty-eight hours with your father."

Dora ordered her martini with her lunch. She always enjoyed a good martini.

"May I ask," she said to her grandson, "how all this came to pass?"

"Come on, Gran," he said, narrowing his eyes. "You know how girls get pregnant."

"I'm not sure I know how teenage girls get pregnant by boys who don't even love them," she said. The martini was perfect, dry and cold.

"Love," he said, practically spitting out the word. "What good is loving someone? Then they die, or leave, or don't love you back. Big deal."

"Well," Dora said, "everyone is going to die. Even you. That's one of humankind's most foolish ideas, that everyone will die except you."

"You know what my mother says about you?" Peter said, narrowing his eyes again. "She says you're a tough old bird. Cold hearted too."

Dora rolled her eyes. "How would Melinda know anything about me at all? As far as I can tell she was in a drug-induced haze until my son died. Then she got scared enough to straighten herself out, go to law school, and join the real world." She leaned across her sandwich and added, "Am I cold hearted because I call things as I see them?"

Peter smiled. She was almost starting to like the boy. "Not at all." He sighed. "I guess maybe I do love Rebecca a little. I mean, I love being with her and everything. Touching her and stuff."

"Yes, well, that's obvious," Dora said, blushing a little. "You know, Tillie, your Aunt Tillie, I mean, got herself in similar trouble. Of course, she was older, in college, and she came home for Christmas with the news. I said, Tillie, you are far too young and immature to have a baby. I'll arrange an abortion for you and that was that. Of course, Tillie agreed."

Peter said, his mouth full of hamburger, "I thought she was . . . you know . . ."

"A lesbian. Yes. Apparently that wasn't always the case."

Peter swallowed and then looked at Dora, all seriousness. "Boy, you've had a sad life, haven't you?"

Dora finished her martini. "Not at all. If you asked anyone about their life when they were seventy-eight years old it would be full of the same sorts of stories. I guarantee you. This baby of yours that's getting born is just one of many blips in your lifetime."

"But it breaks my heart," Peter said.

"What does?" Dora asked him, surprised.

"That I'll never even lay eyes on it. That I'll grow old with a child in the world that I don't even know. That I'm losing something important."

Without warning, Dora felt tears spring to her eyes. Hastily, she closed them and pressed her fingers to her eyelids, hoping her grandson did not see her do it.

"I THOUGHT YOU said it took forever!" Peter shouted.

Dora was surprised to see his cheeks wet with tears, surprised that he would cry so freely.

"I'm sorry," she said, and her own voice sounded weak and feeble.

Peter stood in the middle of the kitchen, still rumpled from sleep. His thin cotton striped pajamas and the way his cowlick stood straight up like a miniature bale of hay made him seem like a child rather than a young man who had just become a father.

"Sorry? That's all you can say?"

His hands were placed on his hips, his jaw jutted out. Dora thought of Dan, how he would stand in this very spot in this very way and challenge her. The thought made her dizzy enough to drop, sighing, into a chair and hold her head in her hands.

"Her mother said she had it yesterday afternoon," Peter was saying, his voice bordering on shrill. "The kid's already like a day old practically."

Dora shook her head. He would never see this child of his anyway. Hadn't he told her that the girl wasn't even going to hold it? That the adopting parents would be right there, waiting, ready to take the baby away with them?

"What can it possibly matter," Dora said evenly, "that you got the news twelve hours after the fact?"

"Almost a day later!" he insisted.

Slowly, Dora stood and made her way to the stove to put on the kettle. She didn't like noise and discussion before she'd had her cup of Earl Grey. She never had. When the children were still at home she would wake up early, make her tea, then slip back into bed to drink it quietly. Now here she was at a time in her life when she should not have to get screamed at and be accused right in her own kitchen, before she'd had her tea.

She concentrated on the kettle, the way it shook slightly as the water began to heat.

"You haven't told me what she had," Dora said.

A puff of steam rose from the spout, then the low whistle began.

Peter's voice was soft now. "A boy," he said, as if he couldn't believe it himself.

A sharp pang of regret shot through Dora's gut. A baby boy. Her Dan's grandson. Her own great-grandchild. She tried to keep her hand steady as she poured the boiling water into her mug, a lumpy thing that Tillie had made in a pottery class some years ago. For an instant Dora believed that she would turn around and find *her* children there: Dan's face still creased from sleep, his frown deep, Tillie's sunnier self humming tunelessly. She would turn, Dora let herself think, and her children would ask for French toast and quarters for treats after school and their mittens and erasers for their pencils and hair ribbons and papers that needed signing. She took a breath and spun around expectantly. But of course there was just this other boy. Peter. Still crying, his face blotchy and swollen now, he waited for something from her, something she could not possibly give him.

DORA DID NOT know what to do for Peter, who moved around the house noisily, slamming cabinets shut, muttering to himself. He called the girl constantly, as if she could give him answers. Dora heard him say: "But they were cool, right? Like in their pictures?" And: "They seemed in love, right? Like they're not going to get divorced, right?" Another time she heard him asking softly: "Did he have any hair? Did he look at you or anything?" It took Dora a moment to understand Peter was asking about his baby, not the man who adopted him.

After several days of this, Peter appeared in front of her as she dozed over a mystery novel.

"I've got to do something," he said.

Dora stared at him, trying to sort out who exactly he was and why he was standing in her parlor.

"Peter," she said finally.

"Yeah. Right." He was jumping up and down a little. "I've got to do something."

"Let's go to dinner," Dora said, getting to her feet, even

though a small roasting chicken was defrosting in her kitchen sink.

Once in the car, she couldn't think of where to go. She drove around the city, confused. She didn't really like all this renovation that was going on, the way they rerouted the entire river and made all the roads go in new directions.

"Maybe I should have talked her into keeping it," Peter was saying. "Maybe I should have married her. I mean, I will never see that kid. Ever."

Dora nodded politely. Weybosset Street, Washington, Dorrance. None of them seemed to be in the right place. It was twilight now, and the lights came on unexpectedly, out of nowhere.

"I mean," Peter said, "it's like he vanished."

"Yes," Dora said. "Well."

Then a thought occurred to her. She and Bill used to take the kids to The Blue Grotto, up on Federal Hill, for special occasions. It had white tablecloths, good martinis, chicken marsala and spaghetti with bolognese sauce. Tillie liked to get a Shirley Temple there and Dan had a Roy Rogers, both with extra cherries.

"Do you like Italian food?" Dora said, getting her bearings.

"Like the Olive Garden?"

Dora sighed. She didn't know what the boy was talking about most of the time. "I suppose," she said.

Federal Hill, at least, had not changed: it was still impossible to get a parking space. After circling a few times, Dora suggested they park and walk the six or seven blocks to the restaurant.

"Whatever," Peter said.

It was one of those summer nights where in the country you would hear crickets, where the air is so still it makes a person move slower. On the sidewalk, Peter took Dora's arm. His chivalry surprised her.

"Maybe I do love her," he said, his voice full of the resignation a man three times his age might have.

Out of the car, Dora noticed that indeed Federal Hill had changed after all. Now there were Thai and Cambodian restaurants everywhere.

"Let's go in here," Peter said. "What do you say?" He stopped abruptly.

Dora glanced up at the sign, the squiggly lines for letters, the red dragon on the window. She had read once that they ate dogs in Cambodia. She thought of the Blue Grotto, the smell of garlic and tomato.

But Peter was tugging her arm.

"Not there," he said. "Here."

She only had a moment to see where he was leading her before they were inside, and in that moment Dora read the words: BUDDY'S TATTOOS.

MELINDA HAD SAID nothing about tattoos. That was what Dora told herself as Peter explained what a good idea this was. He would commemorate his son's birth. He would have a reminder of him every day for the rest of his life. And if the boy ever decided to try and find him, there would be the proof of his fatherhood right on his arm. Dora listened and looked around. It was exactly what she might expect—a little seedy with its peeling paint and hastily washed linoleum floor, the iron smell of blood mingling with an antiseptic that reminded Dora of hospitals, and an array of customers in leather and metal. The lighting was fluorescent.

"I'll get his name and maybe like a little heart or something," Peter said, jabbing his finger at the wall where available tattoos were displayed.

Dora's eyes drifted past cupids and dolphins and vaguely familiar cartoon characters.

"A heart is nice," she said. She sat on a folding chair, her purse on her lap. Like an old lady, she realized, and tried to strike a more casual pose. "But I didn't know there was a name. Or rather, that we knew the name." She crossed her legs at the ankle, the way she had learned in charm school back in the thirties.

Peter studied a variety of hearts. Broken, intertwined, chubby, pink, red. "It's Daniel," he said, without looking at her. He pointed to one of the hearts and said, "This one's good."

A fat hairy man came into the room from one of the curtained off cubicles. He wore farmer overalls with no shirt underneath. "Who's next here?" he said.

"I am," Dora said firmly. She stood up and smoothed her skirt. "I'm getting the same as him."

The man looked from Dora to Peter. "Fifteen each or two for thirty," he said. He laughed at his own joke, then wiggled his fingers at them. "Come on."

Dora and Peter followed him into one of the cubicles.

"You show him," she told her grandson.

Again Peter pointed to a heart and explained the lettering he wanted for the name. He answered questions about color and size. The man nodded thoughtfully, not unlike a painter Dora had once watched in Paris who sat by the Seine with his easel and tubes of paint. Even when the tattoo man—*tattoo artist*, Dora silently corrected herself—prepared his tools, the needles and dyes and medicated swabs, Dora thought of that French painter, how his nose was peeling and pink from sunburn, the yeasty way he'd smelled, his serious concentration. She had wanted to buy that painting; it had filled her with a longing for things she would never have but always want. Bill had laughed at her, claiming it was simply bad art. They had continued their stroll along the river, Bill reading from the guidebook, pointing at this bridge and that monument, while Dora kept glancing over her shoulder at the man painting.

"You need to take off your sweater," the tattoo artist told Dora gently.

She had put on her jade green cashmere twin set for dinner. Now she slipped off the cardigan almost casually, tossing it on Peter's lap.

Dora closed her eyes and offered the man her arm. She thought of nothing. The first prick of the needle startled her with its burning pain.

"Oh," she said, her eyes flying open.

"The outline's the worst part, Gran," Peter said.

Dora took a breath and closed her eyes again. But each prick of the needle sent fresh tears down her cheeks. She heard herself panting, the way she had when she'd waited too long to get to the hospital to have Dan and arrived crouched on the floor of their Impala, like a wild animal.

"Usually people have a few drinks before they come," the man told her.

"It hurts," Dora managed to say between needlepricks and tears. "It hurts so much."

The pain took over her body, her mind, it invaded every part of her: hot, sharp, constant. Until she was no longer separate from it. Only then could she stop crying, open her eyes, and continue.

AFTER ZANE

AFTER ZANE LEFT, I started to bake. Complicated cakes. Exotic éclairs. Soufflés and meringues and desserts with French names I couldn't pronounce. I bought springform pans and candy thermometers, marzipan and candied violets. Everything I made was beautiful. So beautiful that I took photographs of each creation and hung them on my refrigerator, the way my mother used to hang my kindergarten art.

The thing was, I never ate anything I made. Instead, I gave it away. My obstetrician had told me early on to avoid empty calories. All that sugar—brown and white—all that heavy cream and whipped cream and cream cheese added up to nothing but empty calories.

"This has got to stop," said my best friend, Aurora, between bites of yellow butter cake with milk chocolate ganache frosting.

I was eating a low-fat blueberry yogurt and waiting for my graham cracker pecan crust to chill properly. Outside the wind was blowing puffs of snow around like tumbleweed. I thought of tumbleweed, of prairie women, of being somewhere—anywhere—but Foster, Rhode Island, alone and pregnant. I thought of all those Laura Ingalls Wilder books I used to love as a child. I wanted to be that brave and enduring.

"I MEAN," AURORA was saying, "your neighbors are starting to hide from you. Who needs a different cake every day?"

Now the snow was starting to look like spun sugar. Yesterday I had made a frozen cranberry soufflé with a spun-sugar wreath on top. In fact, it was still sitting out in the snow while I tried to decide what to do with it. As usual, Aurora was right. I was running out of people to give my culinary creations to.

Aurora sighed and wiped some frosting off the rim of her plate with her finger. She had copper hair that fell to her shoulders in perfect ringlets, size six Easy Fit jeans, and just the right amount of freckles. Men did not leave Aurora.

I pointed this out to her.

She licked the frosting from her finger thoughtfully. "Joseph Russo," she said finally, smugly.

"Who?"

"Eighth grade," she said. "Took his ID bracelet back in front of the whole school during assembly. It was so humiliating." She looked panicked for an instant. "Not that you should feel humiliated, Beth," she said. "You should feel . . . angry."

I nodded and went to check my crust. It was perfect.

The wind howled, the snow swirled. Somewhere out there Zane was moving about his life without me. I rested my head against the refrigerator, smack in the center of a photograph of my bourbon pecan pie. It had been, I was told, delicious.

NINE MONTHS AFTER we met, eight months after he first said, "I love you," seven months after we eloped, and six months before our baby was due to be born, Zane left me and went back to his ex-girlfriend, Alice.

"But you don't love her," I reminded him as he packed his car. "You love me."

Zane stopped rearranging boxes long enough to shrug. "I'm having second thoughts, Beth," he said.

"Second thoughts?" I said. "About us?" My mind was shouting instructions at me: Remind him how the two of you wrote your own wedding vows! Say the line that makes you both cry—"We were born together, and together we shall be forevermore." Show him the sonogram pictures!

Since I got pregnant, I did everything slower. Think, move, react. So that before I could say anything, Zane was telling me, "Second thoughts about Alice. Not us."

"Alice?" I said, aware that I was repeating everything he said.

Alice was a piano teacher. Everything about her was long—fingers, hair, even her face. "Horsey," Aurora used to say. "She looks horsey." Then Aurora would whinny. I used to think Alice was a funny name, the name of someone's old maiden aunt. But in the autumn air, coming out of Zane's mouth like that, it sounded sexy.

"This," Zane said, looking sadly around him, at me in my new maternity jeans and our old rented farmhouse and our pumpkin patch bursting with fat bright-orange pumpkins, "it all happened too fast." He was cradling the television set. "I'm sorry," he said.

It was October, one of those glorious autumn days that make a person glad to be alive—blue sky, leaves on fire with color, cornstalks and jack-o'-lanterns on doorsteps. Just the day before, Zane and I had walked through the woods that stretched behind our land, had thrown ourselves down on the fallen pine needles and gazed up at the setting sun. Zane had rested his hand on my stomach. Now, standing on our doorstep, hugging myself, I wondered if even then he knew he was leaving.

I watched him close the trunk, check for his car keys, then move toward the driver's seat. I had watched him do these small tasks countless times, mornings as we both went off to work and weekend afternoons when he left to run errands. But all those times I knew he would be back.

He got in the car and adjusted the rearview mirror.

"Zane!" I called. I willed my legs to run after him, but they remained frozen in place.

He rolled down the passenger window and leaned toward it.

Having his attention like that, I couldn't think of anything to say. But as he began to put the car in gear, I yelled, "Together we shall be forevermore! Remember?"

But it was too late. He was already driving away.

ZANE AND ALICE had been together for almost nine years. When they broke up, Alice got the Volvo, their split-level ranch in the suburbs, and their old dog, Bud. Zane got a 1982 Subaru with body rot and a pale-pink-and-mint-green-flowered sofa bed. Alice liked pastels and small floral patterns. Colorless, Aurora called her. Then she'd say, "She's ecru, she's taupe. You, Beth, are purple. Bright purple."

When Zane left me, he left the sofa bed behind. Like most things since I got pregnant, it made me feel nauseous. I hated that sofa bed. I hated pink, except in extreme cases like Pepto-Bismol. When I first went back inside after Zane drove off, I tried sitting in the family room. But that sofa bed glared at me, mocking. Upstairs, our bed with its happy rumpled sheets made me feel like crying. So I went back outside and stretched out on our front lawn. I stayed there, not thinking, until it got dark and the Milky Way appeared above me.

Then I went inside and called Aurora. It wasn't until I heard her casual "Hello" that I started to cry.

ALL THE BAKING had begun with those pumpkins in our yard. Whenever I tried to carve happy faces on them, I ended up with jack-o'-lanterns that looked like the Elephant Man. Finally, I threw out the ghoulish shells and tried to figure out what to do with all the leftover pumpkin flesh. *Pies,* I thought. Ten pies, four dozen pumpkin cookies, and six loaves of pumpkin-spice bread later, I was a baking maniac. Now it was winter, and I had moved on to holiday baking— eggnog cheesecake, Swedish sugar cookies, Noel date bars.

"What you need," Aurora told me as she nibbled a lemon-hazelnut *biscotto*, "is to make lists."

"Lists," I repeated. In the past when my heart was broken, I would drink jug zinfandel and eat lots of chocolate. This time, I couldn't do either. I concentrated on my gingerbread people. Man, woman, child, all with happy icing clothes and wiggly smiles. A happy family.

Aurora wiped the crumbs from her chin and pulled out a pad and pen. "You need a lawyer. You need child support." She glanced at my bulging stomach. "You need a birthing partner," she said. She was starting to scare me. "*Wait*," I said. "You're assuming he's not coming back."

She cleared her throat, then patted my arm. "How could he choose someone so horsey over you? How could he choose a woman who buys furniture from furniture showrooms? You have Mexican antiques! You have folk art! You have style!"

That was when I really started to cry. I had everything, I thought, feeling the strange flutterings of our baby's first movements. Everything except Zane.

WHEN I MET Zane, he and Alice had just split up. I had just split up with my boyfriend, Matthew, and had gone to Boston for the day to shop. Zane was in Crate and Barrel buying glassware. I was buying dishes. He came up to me, holding a wine goblet as if he were making a toast. "Your dishes," he said, "and my glasses make a good combination."

Zane was tall and blond, like a guy in a toothpaste ad. He looked *too* good: I was suspicious. But by the time we left the store and went for Italian food at the kind of restaurant people in movies go to—red-and-white-checked tablecloths, a candle dripping from a chianti bottle, a waiter whispering, "Ah . . . *amore*!" my suspicions had gone the way of all the wine and fettuccine Alfredo we'd had.

"Do you believe in love at first sight?" Zane asked me that night as he left me at my front door.

"Absolutely not," Aurora told me the next morning when I told her the story. "Love at first sight is a myth. A line."

The next time I saw Zane, we sat in my bathtub until our skin wrinkled, and told each other our life stories. He told me about Alice. I told him about Matthew. We discovered we both liked Indian food. We both loved the Isle of Skye. We both knew all the lines to *The Graduate* by heart. We both wanted to move to the country and have babies.

"Alice got indigestion from beef vindaloo," Zane said, nuzzling my neck.

"Matthew said he could never be more than three miles from a building over ten stories high," I told him.

"Alice thought Skye was too cold and rainy."

"Matthew can never stay awake long enough to see when Benjamin and Elaine Robinson have their date," I said.

Then Zane said exactly what I was thinking. "Beth," he whispered, "we're perfect for each other."

"You're nuts," Aurora told me, as I packed all my belongings into liquor store boxes. "You've known this guy a week?"

I didn't have a logical answer. All I could do was hum "Mrs. Robinson."

FOR THOSE FIRST few months after Zane left, I thought about how foolish I had been. I was glad Aurora never said, "I told you so." I walked around our old farmhouse and touched our things to remind myself these past months had been real. Here were our beeswax candles, our wreaths of dried herbs, our wedding vows framed in wood.

Sometimes, after I made my rounds, traveling from room to room and touching everything, I sat on the sofa bed I hated and tried to picture Zane with Alice, the two of them tucked under a pastel quilt, their golden retriever at their feet and a Duraflame log burning in their fireplace. Sometimes I even tried to imagine Matthew, who had moved to Los Angeles after we broke up.

But mostly I thought about the life Zane and I were supposed to be having. We had talked about taking a week off from work and flying to the Bahamas. We had talked about having all our friends over for Thanksgiving. We had chosen names for our baby—Benjamin after the hero of *The Graduate,* Skye after our favorite place in the world. I walked around and whispered those names like a mantra that would bring Zane back.

He called every week, but I never picked up the phone. Let him miss me, I thought as I listened to his voice on the answering machine. He sounded the same. Would you buy toothpaste from this man? I asked myself. Would you elope with him? Would you have his baby? When I rewound the tape, I always tried to imagine him here with me, with his bright white smile. But I could only picture him in a snapshot I once saw of him and Alice. In it, he is smiling, staring straight at the camera. She stands beside him, her hair pulled back in a ponytail, her face serious, her fingers locked together like a church steeple in that child's game.

Aurora said, "There's no way you're spending New Year's Eve alone."

I had spent Christmas with my family, flown to St. Louis clutching jars filled with tiny star-shaped spice cookies, the lids tied with festive plaid ribbons. Everyone had eyed my baked goods suspiciously. They knew I was good for a basic spaghetti sauce, a pot of chili—but tiny cookies? Plaid ribbons? They all thanked me and averted their eyes.

When I got back to Rhode Island, there were two big packages from Zane wrapped in shiny paper on my doorstep. A plush stuffed panda for the baby. An antique silver Mexican tray for me. I put them both in the trash and didn't go back outside until the garbagemen took them away.

"This will not do," Aurora said. She went to each window and opened the blinds, letting in the glaring winter sun. "I'm getting you a blind date for this party."

"He'd better be blind," I muttered, looking down at my stomach. At my last visit, the doctor had smiled and said, "Twenty weeks and your fundus measures twenty. Everything's perfect."

"Hey," Aurora said, "some men find pregnant women very attractive."

"Zane didn't."

"Zane," she said, rolling her eyes.

"Do you think he'll come back?" I asked, trying to sound like it didn't matter.

"Beth," Aurora said, planting herself directly in my line of vision, "do you really want this guy back?"

"Of course not," I lied.

WHILE I DRESSED for the party, I wondered what was wrong with me. Why did I, deep down, still want Zane back? Pride? Revenge? The baby? I remembered how I had broken up with Matthew with such confidence. How I had been so firm and sure.

I squeezed into some black velvet leggings, size large, and looked in the mirror. My blind date was named Arnie. "Think of Arnie Becker on *L.A. Law*," Aurora had told me. "Then the name won't seem so bad." I wondered what Alice and Zane were doing tonight. An image of Alice in something slinky and Zane in a silk smoking jacket, champagne bubbles floating around them, came into my head. I decided to go downstairs and put the finishing touches on the cake I was bringing to the party.

By the time I was done, the doorbell was ringing. Arnie had arrived. He had a chic short ponytail and a bow tie. He taught at Brown and lived on the East Side. "It's one of those historic houses," he said, doing a bad imitation of humble. "Little brass plaque out front. Et cetera." One thing was for certain, Arnie liked himself. A lot. All I had to do was smile and nod from time to time.

By the end of the night, he had drifted into a corner

with a woman named Chloe who modeled. "Catalogue work," she'd said, sounding very much like Arnie. I sat alone on the sofa and ate carrot sticks, watching Arnie and Chloe whisper together while everyone else dug into my chocolate mousse cake.

Aurora plopped down beside me. She wore a glittery minidress.

"Arnie's a jerk," she said.

I nodded. We both watched him rub his nose against Chloe's, like an Eskimo.

"This time next year," Aurora said, "you'll have a great little baby and nothing else will matter."

I was growing very tired of Aurora's advice. It wasn't midnight yet, but I didn't care. All I wanted was to go home and crawl into bed. I stood and thanked Aurora for everything.

She looked puzzled. "But it's not next year yet," she said.

"It's close enough," I told her.

WHEN I GOT home, Zane was sitting at the kitchen table eating some white chocolate macadamia cookies I had baked.

"Are you here for an affair?" I said, surprised at how quickly I could retrieve a line from *The Graduate,* at how well I was keeping my cool.

"You don't answer my calls," he said. "I miss you."

I chewed on my bottom lip, eating off the remnants of the lipstick I'd worn to the party. I wanted him back so badly my knees were shaking. "You look beautiful," Zane said.

"Where's Alice? I mean, New Year's Eve and all that."

Zane finished off another cookie before he answered. "We're discussing our relationship," he said finally. "What was good. What was bad. Why it turned sour."

"Isn't that all old news? When I met you, you two had broken up. A fait accompli."

"She knows how much I love you. We're both taking some time to think. To decide."

I squeezed my eyes shut so I didn't have to look at him. *He isn't coming back*, I told myself.

"Beth?" Zane said softly.

I opened my eyes. "I don't want to see you until you've made up your mind," I said.

Later, I was shocked at my firmness. I lay alone in our bed, feeling our baby roll and tumble, and wondering where I'd gotten the strength to throw Zane out when what I really wanted was to wrap myself around him and never let go.

AFTER THE SNOW melted and spring threatened, the rain came, turning our backyard into mud. I spent my weekends buying baby clothes, tiny things called Onesies and Sleepers. I refinished a crib, painted plump animals in bright primary colors on the walls of the nursery, interviewed nannies.

I still baked, but now it was simple things—sugar cookies for Valentine's Day, apple pie, pound cake. Aurora missed the fancy stuff, but my neighbors seemed relieved. "Oh, spice cake! How wonderful!" Mrs. Grady told me. Things were starting to change.

The only thing that remained constant was that I was still waiting for Zane to make up his mind. Sometimes when he called, I almost picked up the phone. Almost, but I resisted. Instead, I did my prenatal Jane Fonda exercises and practiced my breathing.

"A spring baby is the best kind," Aurora told me. She was my birthing partner, and after class she always came over for coffee and dessert.

"Guess what?" she said, nibbling on her oatmeal cookie. "Arnie and Chloe are getting married."

"So soon?"

Our eyes met for an instant.

"You know," Aurora said, "sometimes, maybe there is such a thing as love at first sight. What do I know? I've had sixteen boyfriends in eight years." She caught my gaze again. "You never know."

"That's for sure."

"I think he's going to come back," Aurora said. "How could he not? He's just being a typical man. Considering his options. Stuff he should have done first."

WHEN ZANE DID come back, it was raining. Hard. I had just frosted a dozen chocolate cupcakes and sprinkled them with multicolored jimmies. Outside, our yard was bursting with life—bright crocuses and tulips, lime green buds on the tips of tree branches. My due date was two weeks away, and everything was ready.

I heard Zane's car pull up, heard him swear as he stepped into some mud. I was upstairs, getting ready for bed. I went to the window and watched as he made the slippery route back home.

He rang the doorbell. But instead of answering it, I opened the window and pressed my face to the screen. The rain felt warm against my skin.

"Hi," I said.

Zane stepped back to get a good look at me. He didn't have on a raincoat or hat, and water streamed down his face, matted his hair to his head.

"Let me in," he said. "It's pouring."

"What do you want?" I called down. "I was just going to bed."

"You, Beth," He said. I could see his dazzling smile even from that distance, even in the dark and rain. "I want you."

I stared down at him. He looked, I thought, very small.

"Beth," he said. "Come on. I'm soaked."

But all I did was shake my head.

"Come on," he said again, leaning his head back to try to see me more clearly.

"Zane," I said, "I don't know if I want you to come back."

He laughed. "Very funny," he said. When I didn't answer, he shouted, "What about our baby? What about us?"

"I don't know," I told him, which was only half true. I felt certain about the baby, but about us I really didn't have a clue. "I guess I need some time. To think. To decide."

"But I love you," he said.

"I know," I said. Then I stepped back from the window.

He stood out there a very long time. But finally, I heard the car door slam shut, the tires spin in the mud, then Zane driving away. That was when I made my way downstairs, into the kitchen. My cupcakes were lined up, shining with chocolate and colorful sprinkles. I removed the plastic wrap and sank my teeth into a cupcake. In the morning, I would call Aurora, I would practice my breathing, I would pick a bouquet of spring flowers. But for right then, I wanted nothing more than to sit and enjoy what I had made. It had been too long since I'd had something that sweet.

JOELLE'S MOTHER

SHE MUST BE beautiful, the three of us thought. Not like our mother or the mothers of our friends with their long tangle of hair and arms lined with silver bracelets from Mexico. But beautiful like Joelle herself, all matching sweater sets and small pearl earrings and hair tamed by a fat headband. In our school, we did not have girls like Joelle. Instead of plaid skirts with a big gold pin on the side and loafers, we wore long flowered dresses, clogs from Sweden. Exotic, we thought, whenever we saw Joelle, our stepsister, again.

She made us lose our breath when we caught that first sight of her stepping, bored, from the train once a month. She came to visit our father who was her father too; it was our mothers who were different. We would run to Joelle with such ferocious hugs she almost lost her balance. Joelle was not a hugger, but she let us hug her and hang on the sleeve of her cardigan, dragging her toward our mother who waited by the car. For those few minutes, we had Joelle to ourselves. We breathed in her scent: Christmas trees. We babbled, the three of us talking at once about the total eclipse or the new Italian phrases we'd learned or how a snake sheds its skin. Joelle kept her eyes straight ahead, nodded if we were lucky. She let us guide her through the train station and outside.

Our mother waved at us, standing beside our VW, the one that could not make a steep hill so our mother had to get out and push, letting one or two of us steer. Also, the heater never worked so in winter we kept our mittens on, even inside the car. Joelle's mother drove a Ford of some kind. We knew because Joelle told us; her mother always drove Fords.

In those moments, wrapped in Joelle's scent, bursting from the train station, and seeing our mother there, disappointment and embarrassment flooded us. Joelle's mother did not want her to speak Italian, did not have hard bottoms of her feet from going barefoot, did not have long dark hair under her arms or candles stuck into empty wine bottles made thick from melted wax. Our mother grinned and waved and whistled through an O made with her fingers stuck beneath her tongue, shrill and loud. She always mussed up Joelle's hair, first thing. She always said, *Time to let your hair down now!*

The three of us piled into the back of the VW. Joelle sat straight as a ruler up front. Our mother put on "Suite: Judy Blue Eyes" too loud, then shouted at Joelle about our weekend plans. We shrank into the back seat, not wanting to hear. Our weekends were always the same: Friday night potlucks that ended in everyone dancing and drunk in our tiny square yard. Saturday afternoon drives from our house in Baltimore to Washington where we had to look at paintings or mummies or dinosaur bones. Then Chinese at Mr. Hsu's on P Street. Sundays meant long walks somewhere, by the harbor or in the park, maybe crabs for dinner. Why our mother had to say all of this to Joelle, who knew it as well as we did, we could not understand. Joelle stared out the window while our mother shouted over Crosby, Stills and Nash.

We pretended our mother disappeared and we were sent to live in the suburbs with Joelle and her mother. Our mother made us eat yogurt at lunchtime. Also raisins, dried figs, Brazil nuts. But not Joelle's mother. She bought her TV dinners, Salisbury steak or turkey with stuffing, all four courses nestled in their own private compartments. We imagined a dishwasher, a swimming pool—built-in. We imagined bedspreads light as angels' wings, white or maybe baby blue. We counted all the Fords we passed, and sighed.

IN A CIGAR BOX that had long ago been painted black and covered with seashells glued onto it crookedly lay evidence of our father's former life with Joelle's mother. A wedding band, thick and gold, a lock of hair, also thick and gold, the only remnants of our father's past. We thought him mysterious. A golden-haired first wife, a daughter, a life he talked about only when we pushed him.

How did you meet Joelle's mother?

How did you fall in love?

Where did you get married? Did she wear a long satin dress? Our mother didn't. Hers was white, Mexican, cotton, embroidered. She stood barefoot on a beach in Delaware. They blew conch shells, wore wedding rings fashioned from seaweed, had their friend Raymond play the flute. We knew Joelle's mother wouldn't stand for any of that. We had proof: the solid gold ring. Inside, in scrolly letters, initials carved beside a date. June 6, 1966. A million years ago.

"Another lifetime," our father told us, sighing heavily.

But we pushed and prodded, hungry for details.

"We met in college," he told us finally. "Are you satisfied?"

Satisfied? We were starving.

"Why didn't you stay married to her?" we asked. Unspoken between us was our fantasy—then she would be our mother too.

"If I had, then none of you monkeys would be born," our father said, leveling his gaze at us, the one he used in his lectures at Johns Hopkins; he was a professor of English literature. "You are one part me and one part your mother."

Guiltily, we left him to his blue books for grading.

But he called to us, and we turned back to face him.

"It's about love, you know," he said. "I thought I loved her, but I didn't. Your mother," he added, "your mother I adore. For always."

Of course, we asked Joelle. *Did our father live with you and your mother? Did he make up stories for you at night? Did he hold your mother's hand? Kiss her on the back of the neck while she stood stirring soup on the stove?*

Joelle was stingy with details. Sometimes she would bark at us. "No, he never did any of those things. He left us, you know!" We would sulk out of her room and whisper about what that meant. Could he leave us too someday? Then we would study our father for signs of his possible departure. But he remained the same, slightly goofy and distracted, circling our mother with nervous attention. Other times Joelle would cry and blame our mother for ruining their life. We thought our mother capable of ruining lives, with her strong opinions and the certainty with which she did everything. But Joelle and her mother's life hardly seemed ruined. Still, when we raised this point to Joelle she would only shake her head and refuse to elaborate.

Once in a while Joelle would tell us something that we wanted to know, how our father and her mother had honeymooned in Bermuda in a big hotel with a pink sand beach. We could not, of course, imagine it: our father at a resort, lounging on the beach, sipping rum swizzles and slathering Joelle's mother's back with coconut oil. But she told us it was true; she had seen pictures. When we begged Joelle to bring the pictures to us she grew quiet, sullen. "My mother," she told us, "would kill me if I did that."

Our mother, we knew, would never go to Bermuda. We looked it up in the atlas and stared at the tiny island with the pink sand beaches where everyone spoke in British accents and stopped midafternoon for teatime. One night we asked her, feigning innocence, if we could take a vacation to Bermuda. We waited, breaths held, for her reply. "Why in the world would we ever go there?" she said, wrinkling her nose as if she smelled something very very bad.

JOELLE IN SUMMER was best. She arrived in cool tennis whites, tanned from days spent at The Club swimming or taking lessons of one kind or another. We made her tell us details of The Club. Our summer days were spent sitting on the sidewalk trying to finish our Popsicles before they melted. Or running under someone's sprinkler. Or taking turns standing in front of the fan in the kitchen. For two weeks every year our parents rented a cottage at Rehoboth

Beach. Then we rode waves, collected fireflies in empty may-
onnaise jars, ate watermelon on the screened in porch. We
waited all summer for those two weeks. Until then, we had
Joelle's descriptions of The Club.

"No one can yell there," she told us. "Suppose your
mother wants you to come out of the pool. Maybe it's time
to go home. Or maybe she wants you to go with her to The
Grill for a hamburger. She has to walk to the edge of the pool
and get you. No yelling from the chaise lounge."

She pronounced chaise, *chezz*. We imitated her, taking
turns being Joelle's mother. Sit on the chezz, we'd say. Now
walk to the very edge of the pool and ask us politely to come
out for lunch. This game always ended in a fight: everyone
wanted to be Joelle's mother all the time.

We made her tell us more. What kind of bathing suits did
people wear at The Club?

"One piece," Joelle said. "Or a two piece that doesn't
show your belly button."

She explained that intermittent belly buttons were okay.
That was when a woman walked and her belly button
showed sometimes. But full out belly buttons were prohib-
ited. The rule applied to kids as well. Embarrassed, we did
not mention the way our mother sunbathed topless in our
backyard, the way she said *chase* lounge, the way she stood
on the front porch of our row house and yelled above the
noisy crickets for us to come inside. Instead of nightly games
of kick the can, we forced our neighbors to play our version
of tennis or golf, using branches of trees and old musty balls
from someone's basement. Joelle only watched, sitting on
our stoop, high above us, her sneakers so white they glowed.

OUR NAMES—Molly, Sarah, Hannah—were common and dull. Not at all like Joelle, which sounded exotic, practically French. In every class or every house for one square block, there resided another Molly, another Sarah, another Hannah. But we never met another Joelle. We took this naming of us as still one more betrayal.

"What were you thinking?" we asked our mother.

"I was thinking of lovely little girl names," she said, "for my lovely little girls."

We told her our names were horrid, ugly, everywhere.

"Should I have named you Tallulah?" she asked us. "Hermione? What?"

"Something fancy," we said sadly. "Something like Joelle."

WHEN EXACTLY THE phone calls began, we could never pinpoint. It seemed that one summer they were suddenly there, the tinny ring of our black telephone, then the hushed voices, the tears, the slam of Joelle's bedroom door, my father placating, pleading. Sometimes we huddled in the hall-way, trying to hear what was being said, but the words always sounded vague and muddled behind the closed doors. Sometimes we came upon Joelle whispering into the tele-phone. She would glare at us and stop talking until we left the room. Then, our ears pressed against the door, we would try to make out what exactly she was saying.

Our mother grew silent and edgy. Whenever the phone rang she jumped as if she'd been shot, then answered it softly, turning her head away from us. More than once we stumbled inside from the blazing Baltimore heat for more Popsicles or to complain about how bored and hot we'd grown, to find her sitting at our big wooden kitchen table, crying.

All summer, this went on, until we stopped thinking about it and accepted it as part of the grown-up world our parents inhabited. Instead we focused on other things: stringing long strands of beads to hang in our doorway, monitoring the growth of a litter of newborn kittens who resided in our neighbor's garage, begging our mother for one of those kittens, counting the days until we finally left the city and went to our rented cottage in Rehoboth Beach. We traded 45s with our friends. We made up dances—the Frog and the Cobra. We pretended our backyard was The Club, and threw out anyone who yelled there. We begged our mother for some of the little white socks Joelle always wore, ankle length with pastel pom-poms on the backs, and when she finally relented, we wore them day after day, with the sticks and the musty balls, practicing our golf and tennis.

The weekend we were finally leaving for the beach, Joelle arrived at our house with our father. She had her lovely suntanned arms folded tightly across her chest and whenever we spoke to her she turned her head, lifting it upward so her nose pointed at the ceiling. We all begged her to talk to us. But she wouldn't, not to us or our father or our mother, who walked around looking as tight as the blue metal top we liked to spin across the kitchen floor.

At a sullen dinner on the screened in porch, we tried to entice her with plans for the beach. Last year, we reminded her, we had found a jellyfish. We talked about the french fries available there, salty and greasy and hot. We told her that Hurricane Margaret was headed north from Puerto Rico. We might have to get masking tape and make X's for our windows. The waves, we said, would be tall. Maybe even a hundred feet high.

"Shut up," Joelle told us. They were the first words she'd spoken all day, and they flew out of her mouth like gunfire. "Just shut up. All of you."

In a flash our mother was out of her seat and leaning right into Joelle's face. "Don't you ever say that to my children again. Ever. Do you understand? I have had enough of you. Of this. Do you hear me?"

We stared at the two of them, silent and unsure of who to hate—Joelle for telling us to shut up, or our mother for offending Joelle. We did not know what to do or what might happen next. It seemed like right then a car screeched up to our house, but maybe that was some time later. A car did screech up that night, its door flying open and banging shut. We heard the unfamiliar sound of high heels pounding up our front walk.

Then just one word, spoken into the hot summer air: "Joelle."

We looked through the screen, where moths clung, batting their gossamer wings, and saw Joelle's mother standing on the steps that led to our house, her arms folded in such a way that she appeared to be hugging herself. In the glare of the single bulb that hung over the front stairs, we could make out every detail. She was the tallest woman we had ever seen, or so she seemed standing there like that. Her hair, no longer golden, was pulled into a tight chignon, and everything she wore matched: pale yellow pants and tunic top, large wooden earrings painted red and yellow, with matching large wooden beads around her neck. She had on nylons under the wide legs of her pants, and high heels in a color we would later call taupe, but then thought of as the color of flesh. Her lips and cheeks were pink.

Everything about her shocked us. But mostly what we saw was that she was not, as we had thought, beautiful. At least not in the soft and exotic way we had imagined. She looked like women we saw pushing carts at the Safeway, choosing fruits and vegetables with care. She looked like anyone, different than our mother, but not the extraordinary, magical woman we had hoped. She was simply a mother—someone else's mother at that.

We all—the three of us, our parents, and Joelle—stayed seated on the red folding chairs at the red card table, our plates full of our mother's famous couscous salad, the one with cucumbers and kalamata olives, and feta cheese; the one she always took to potluck suppers. Joelle's mother spoke again. "Joelle," she said, in a cool voice, "come on now." We could imagine that voice at The Club, floating across the shimmering blue of the swimming pool, beckoning Joelle to her. We could imagine it whispering good night. But we could not then understand the power in that voice. With those few words it took Joelle away from us and changed our lives.

Joelle stood, but it was our mother who stepped outside. "Please," she said to Joelle's mother. "Let's not do this. Not in front of my girls. I don't want them upset by any of this. Let's go inside with Hal and talk like adults."

"I've talked all summer," Joelle's mother said. "She doesn't want to come here anymore. She wants to come home."

This shocked us. Later, the three of us hot and sweaty in our bed, our legs tangled together, we would try to sort it out, how all of those whispered phone calls had been pleas from Joelle to leave us, to not come back. We felt betrayed by Joelle, by her mother, by the things we could not even begin to understand.

"After all this time," our mother said, "why can't you let it go? It was all so long ago."

Joelle's mother did not answer her. She just said in her cool voice, "Joelle, let's go. I've come to take you home."

Joelle took the napkin from her lap and folded it into a neat square, then got to her feet. She did not look at any of us, not even our father. She just walked away, past us, past her own mother who stood in the same pose Joelle had held all day, arms folded across her chest, face turned upward so that her nose pointed toward the ceiling. Joelle opened the screen door carefully and stepped outside, into the hot August night.

Our father was on his feet now too, but somehow we understood that this was between our mothers—Joelle's and ours. We understood the way it was, that Joelle would always belong to her mother, and we would always belong to our mother. The adults said things, but we were no longer listening. Instead, we let the realization that we could not have a different mother, that we belonged to this one, settle in. Joelle and her mother walked down our path, side by side, to their Ford and we watched them drive away from us.

Eventually, of course, Joelle would visit again, awkwardly at first and then slowly with a confidence and understanding that somehow she straddled two families, two lives. She never again seemed as mysterious as she had before that summer night. In the way that children have, we put aside that which we could not have or comprehend and let both Joelle and her mother become ordinary in our eyes. They both lost the hold on us they used to have and instead developed into two separate people, fixtures in our lives in different ways, but firmly a part of us: the big sister with a different mother, our father's ex-wife.

As for us that August, we went to the beach, where we brought our mother perfect shells that we collected along the shore. In the sunshine there she seemed to grow beautiful. Had her hair always had that particular wave to it? And wasn't the way her front teeth overlapped interesting? We wore the new bikinis she had bought for us, and brightly colored rubber flip-flops, and wreaths of black-eyed Susans. Every chance we had, we hugged our mother tight. We whispered that we loved her because we did, irrevocably, unconditionally, eternally. *We don't want any mother but you,* we assured her, and ourselves. It was August and hot and summer was coming to an end. Even there, at the shore, we could smell autumn approaching. We could feel its chill in the air, sending goosebumps up our arms at night. Our mother pulled us into her arms and held us, thankfully, close.

ESCAPES

WHAT I DO with my niece Jennifer is this. I ride the cable cars again and again, paying four dollars each time. She is fourteen and gets a thrill hanging off the side of the car as it plunges down San Francisco's steep hills. She says it is like flying, and indeed the wind does pick up her Esprit scarf, the one decorated with purple and yellow palm trees, and tosses it stiffly backward in the same way that Charles Lindbergh's scarves appear in old flying photos of him.

I take her to Candlestick Park for the Giants' last game of the season and sit shivering under an old blanket I bought in Mexico long ago. Jennifer does not understand baseball, but I try to explain it to her. Three outs to an inning, nine innings to a game, the importance of a good shortstop. But she does not get it. When Chris Sabo of the Reds strikes out she says, "Caryn, why is it still their turn? You said three outs to an inning."

"But three strikes," I tell her, "is just one out." Jennifer shakes her head and closes her eyes for the rest of the game. Even when I nudge her and say, "Look! A home run!" she keeps her eyes closed, does not move.

We spend an entire day at the Esprit factory outlet. Jennifer fills a shopping cart with bargains. She is tall, like her father, my brother, was. She is fourteen and already almost six feet, and so thin that her hip bones poke out from her faded blue jeans. She does not have to wear a bra. She keeps her hair long, so that it flies around her head like a golden cloud. One of the saleswomen asks Jennifer if she is a model. "Me?" Jennifer says, confused, embarrassed. She slouches even more than usual and shakes her yellow hair. Then she walks away. But when we go into the dressing room and she sees that there is no privacy, no curtains or doors, that everyone is standing half-naked in front of mirrors, Jennifer leaves her shopping cart and walks out of the store without trying on a thing.

What I do not do is mention Jennifer's arms. Tiny uneven scars creep up her wrists like a child's sloppy cross-stitch. She wears long-sleeved blouses, and dozens of tiny bracelets, but still the scars peek through. I pretend that Jennifer's wrists are as smooth as the rest of her. That the scars are not even there. I don't ask her any questions about it. Instead, I take her to the Top of the Mark at sunset. I bring her to Seal Rock where we stare through telescopes at the sea lions sunning themselves.

RIGHT BEFORE JENNIFER came to stay with me, my boyfriend, Luke, left. He said he needed to try his luck in New York. Maybe, he said, he'd become really famous there. Like Laurence Olivier. That was in August and I haven't heard from him since.

Sherry, Jennifer's mother, called me on a Saturday morning in late September and said, "You've got to take her. She's been kicked out of school. Sell her. Adopt her. I don't care. Just take her. I'm going nuts." I looked out my window at the California sky, a bluer, higher sky than anywhere else in the world. Since Luke left, I hadn't done much of anything except swim two miles a day, go to work at the tiny magazine office on Polk Street where I'm a copy editor, and dream of where to escape to next. Sometimes, I rented old movies, ones with Barbara Stanwyck and Joan Crawford in them. Ones that forced me to cry.

While I looked at the sky I thought about my life as a flat straight line like a dead person's heart on a monitor. Sherry told me that Jennifer was really out of hand now. "And I have my studies to worry about," Sherry added. She was in travel-agent school. On weekends, she got to take junkets to Puerto Vallarta and New Orleans.

I had not seen Jennifer in almost two years when Sherry called me that day. My brother David had been dead for almost ten years. So I'm still not sure what made me say yes, I'll take her for a while. Except for maybe the thought of sharing that ultrablue sky with someone seemed so appealing, and the thought of a few bleeps and peaks in my life seemed like a good idea.

Before she hung up, Sherry said, "Don't feel compelled to talk about her cutting her wrists or anything. She wants to put that behind her."

"What?" I said. Had I missed something here? I thought. Jennifer had cut her wrists? They say suicide is contagious and David had done it, hung himself in his jail cell where he was serving time for dealing drugs. "I thought you weren't going to tell her," I told Sherry. We had invented a story when it happened to David. He was in a car accident, we'd decided. He fell asleep at the wheel.

"I didn't," she said. "It must run in your family or something."

"It does not," I said, wishing I had not agreed to take Jennifer. What did I know about teenagers? Or suicide? Or anything at all?

ON FISHERMAN'S WHARF, Jennifer buys more bracelets. They are copper or gold, with tiny beads in the center or chunks of stones, turquoise and amethyst. I wait, bored, gazing at the Golden Gate Bridge while she chooses them from the street vendors that line the sidewalks. She has been with me for two weeks and shows no signs of leaving. Yesterday, she got a postcard from Sherry in Acapulco, written entirely in Spanish. She read it, her face a blank, then tossed it in the trash. "I didn't know you could read Spanish," I told her.

"I can't," Jennifer said.

Jennifer loves all the tourist trap things around the wharf. She spends hours in the souvenir shops and pushing her way through the crowds. She does not smile much, but here her face softens and I almost expect her to break into a grin. David was a great smiler. And so was Sherry. But their daughter's face is set and hard. A mask.

"What's that?" she asks me as we eat our crab cocktails at the crowded food stall. We are crushed against a family of tourists wearing identical pink-and-blue-striped sweatshirts, all fresh-faced and blond.

I look at where she is pointing, across the bay.

"Alcatraz," I tell her.

She frowns. "Alcatraz."

"It was a maximum-security prison."

"Can we go there?" she asks me. Her eyes are topaz. They remind me of a tiger's.

"Maybe next week," I sigh, tired of sightseeing.

"Okay," Jennifer says, fixing her eyes on the hunk of rock in the water. Around her neck, a charm on a chain catches in the sun. A cable car.

"That's pretty," I say. "When did you buy it?"

She looks at me now. "You can have it if you want," she says. She slips the chain over her head and holds it out to me.

"No, that's okay," I tell her.

But she is putting it on me even as I protest. The little gold cable car settles against my collarbone. I feel guilty for not wanting to take her to see Alcatraz and I promise myself we'll definitely go next week. If she hasn't gone home to Miami by then.

I GET A LETTER from Luke in New York. It is written on paper with his initials on the top, and sounds like it is from a stranger. He tells me about the weather there, and how difficult it is to figure out the subway system. He signs the letter "Sincerely, Luke."

"Who's Luke?" Jennifer asks me.

I did not show her the letter, so I figure she has been looking through my things. Somehow, this does not even make me angry. My tiny apartment on Fourth Avenue has been so lonely that the idea of sharing it and everything in it makes me almost happy. For a while, Luke's shirts were crammed into my one closet, his deodorant and toothbrush and comb cluttered my bathroom. Now, Jennifer's things are mingling with mine. When I turn off the bathroom light, her toothbrush glows orange. Her multitude of bracelets are everywhere I look, as if they are actually reproducing.

So I tell her who Luke is without mentioning that she really shouldn't be reading my letters.

"Did you love him?" she asks me.

I only shrug. "Who knows?" I say.

"Did my mother love my father?" she asks then, suddenly.

I answer, "Yes," immediately, but then I wonder about my answer. To me, Sherry and David were like Bonnie and Clyde. They were always doing something illegal. Their apartment was filled with an air of danger. Once, in a kitchen drawer, I saw dozens of stolen credit cards. Their cars disappeared mysteriously. They kept scales and spoons and plastic bags where other people kept pots and pans. How do I know that they loved each other? But Jennifer seems satisfied with my easy answer.

Jennifer says, "Some things don't make sense to me. Like why was my father in a car in Pennsylvania when we lived in Miami? And why aren't there any pictures of us all together?"

"I don't know," I tell her. "I was away at the time." I don't fill in the details, that I was living in St. Thomas, serving tropical drinks and soaking up the sun until my skin turned very brown.

She studies my face for a long time, searching for something that I can't give her.

WHEN SHERRY CALLS I ask her when she will take Jennifer back. "She should go to school," I tell her.

"She'll be expelled again anyway. She steals from kids' lockers, takes whatever she wants. Can you believe it?"

I feel like both Jennifer and Sherry are hiding things from me, giving me little bits and pieces but keeping the big parts to themselves. I try to imagine Sherry in the small pink house she and Jennifer live in. Jennifer has told me that they have orange trees in their backyard, and a plastic pink flamingo on their lawn. I can see Sherry there, in her high-heeled sandals and platinum hair. I used to think she looked exactly like my old Barbie doll, all pointy breasts and tiny waist. Her hair is blond like Jennifer's, but bleached and molded into a tight bubble. That is how I imagine her as she talks to me now, a Barbie doll in her Florida toy house, surrounded by bougainvillea and orange blossoms, staring blankly at a plastic lawn ornament.

"She is nothing but trouble," Sherry is telling me. "Stealing and cheating on tests. She actually copied a *Time* magazine article about Houdini and handed it in as her report on a famous person. Like the teacher wouldn't know someone else wrote it."

Jennifer is stretched out on my couch, lazily flipping through a magazine. She does not seem to be listening to the conversation.

"Well," I ask Sherry, "what's the problem?"

"Who knows? I'm trying to make a better life for us. Travel agents get discount tickets and hotels. We could see the whole world if we wanted to."

Over the years, Sherry has learned many skills. She was a licensed electrologist, removing women's mustaches and shaping their eyebrows. She booked bands for a nightclub and tried her hand at calligraphy. None of it worked as well as her days with David breaking the law.

"I would think she'd want to travel," I say. It was all that I used to want, my way of getting out of tough spots, of leaving men and looking for new ones.

Sherry laughs. "All she wants is to make trouble. But you say she's being good there, so let her stay for a bit more."

I want to explain that I am tired of Jennifer being here. That she is not really helping me decide what to do next. That I have an urge, once more, to pick up and go. To L.A., maybe. Or even Hawaii. Luke signed his letter "Sincerely" and I want to run.

But I say none of these things. I just stare at Jennifer and wonder how she could have actually done it to herself. How she felt when it didn't work. From Miami, Sherry makes excuses for having to hang up. She doesn't ask to speak to her daughter, and I don't offer.

"Wow," Jennifer says when I take her to my tiny, cramped office. "Look at all of these places." She touches the photographs that line my desk and walls and shelves. Pictures of Peru and British Columbia, of people climbing a frozen waterfall and of seals in the Galápagos Islands.

From my window, I can see hookers on the corner, a man drinking something from a paper bag. They call this area of the city the Tenderloin. That sounds gentle to me. Tender loins. This is not a gentle place.

"Have you been to all these places?" Jennifer asks me. She holds out a picture of a dense jungle. She has on a new ring, a thin gold one with two hearts dangling from it.

"No," I tell her. "I just put them in the magazine."

"If I could," she says, still clutching at the jungle photograph, "I would go everywhere. Around the world. I'd even volunteer to go on the space shuttle."

I frown, thinking about Sherry. "When your mother finishes travel-agent school—"

Jennifer laughs. "She'll never finish. She never finishes anything."

"She told me you were expelled from school," I say softly.

Now Jennifer sighs. "I was. I'd rather stow away on a ship than go to school every day. There's nothing there."

"She told me—"

"Whatever she told you is true," Jennifer says firmly.

"Oh."

My eyes drift to her wrists, to her bracelets and beneath them, to her scars.

"Caryn," Jennifer says, "what was he doing in Pennsylvania? What was his job?"

I hesitate. His job was dealing drugs, I say in my mind.

Jennifer laughs again. "My mother says I'm a wild thing. She says I'm like my father." She leans out the open window, too far out. My heart seems to slow down, to freeze. I think, she is jumping from this fifth-floor window but I can't reach out in time to grab her. Then she pulls herself back in, and looks at me as if she didn't just dangle five stories.

"I like looking out," she says. And then she smiles. A smile that makes her face look like it hurts.

SOMEWHERE, I HAVE a map of Hawaii. I will find it, I decide, and study it. I will make plans for a new life in the shadow of a volcano. I've served drinks before at seaside resorts. I can do it again. The names of the islands are magical. Maui and Kauai. For days, the fog here in San Francisco has been thick as mashed potatoes and it is starting to depress me. Every morning, Jennifer is staring at me, waiting for answers. It's time, I think, to move.

I search my drawers, but the map is gone. What I find instead are handfuls of jewelry: the bracelets Jennifer likes to wear, and thick ropes of rose quartz and yellow jade, and earrings made of dangling crystals and rings in all sizes. There is no way that Jennifer could have bought all of this jewelry. Where would she get the money? I lay everything out across my bed, and it sparkles and winks at me in the late afternoon light. Then I put it all away.

THE FOG IS still thick on the day we go to Alcatraz. We wait in line, then crowd onto the ferry. I have paid an extra dollar for us to get the recorded tour, which comes from a bright yellow Walkman and clunky headphones that make us look like Martians. Jennifer is wearing a Cal Berkeley sweatshirt and a boy asks her if she goes there.

"I'm in ninth grade," she tells him.

The boy walks away.

On the island, we walk through the steps that the tour instructs us to take. Stop at the sign that says DINING HALL, we are told. Take a right on Michigan Avenue. Stand under the clock. Look at the pictures on the wall. We do whatever the voice tells us, like robots. Jennifer's tape is two steps ahead of mine, and every time I approach her it seems she has to walk on to somewhere else.

The recorded voice tells us how on New Year's Eve, the prisoners could hear music and laughter from a yacht club across the bay.

We step inside a cell and pretend we are in solitary confinement. All around us, families snap pictures of each other behind bars. I stand in my cell in the dark and close my eyes. The voice tells me about the cold, damp air here. About all the tricks inmates used to help them get through solitary. Throw a button on the floor and try to find it in the dark. Imagine entire movies.

I can feel Jennifer come and stand beside me, I can smell the perfume she wears all the time. She takes my hand in hers.

"Imagine being locked in here and knowing that San Francisco is right across the bay," she says. "Hearing people at a party."

I open my eyes. "But we can walk out," I tell her. "We're not in solitary."

"I know," she says. "But imagine."

We are way behind on our tapes now. And we have to fast forward to catch up. Quickly, Jennifer and I go through the prison, poking our heads into cells and rooms, until we find the rest of the tour. We are at the end, listening to a description of escapes from Alcatraz.

There were many that failed, the voice croons in my ears, and only one that perhaps was successful. I listen to the details of that escape, of how the men collected hair from the barbershop floor to use on papier-mâché masks of their faces. How they dug for months to get through the prison walls to an air shaft. They were never found, the tape tells me.

JENNIFER AND I stand on the top of Alcatraz, looking out. Her hair is blowing wildly in the cold breeze, but she does not try to control it, to hold it down.

"I know you took all that jewelry," I tell her. "I know you stole it."

She doesn't answer me. I cannot see her face under her blowing hair.

Finally, she says, "I like to think they made it."

"Who?"

"Those three men who tried to escape. Maybe one of them didn't drown. Maybe at least one of them is free."

I gaze down the rock to the water pounding the shore. I don't agree with her. I think they must have all died down there.

"About that jewelry," I say.

She turns to me. "Here," she says. "Take it." She unclasps each bracelet, letting them drop into my hands.

"I don't want it," I tell her. "That's not the point."

But she keeps taking them off, until finally she has bare

arms, and all of her crooked scars are revealed. She is standing before me, arms turned upward, naked of all the
turquoise and amethyst and copper.

I take her wrists in my hands, lightly. There are so many
questions I could ask her. So many things I want to know.
But what I realize, standing there, feeling the bumps of her
skin under my hands, is that there really is no escaping. Not
for Sherry, not for Jennifer, not for me. The only thing left to
do is to stick it out.

Jennifer's eyes are set right on me. She says, "If I really
wanted to do it, I would have made the cuts deeper. And up
and down instead of across. No one understands that I knew
the real way. The right way. But I just wanted to see what
would happen, to faint or go away for a little while."

"It's not worth it," I say. "Sooner or later you have to
come back."

She nods. There are tears in her eyes, but they could be
from the stinging salty air, like mine. The ferry is chugging
toward us, and still holding on to each other we slowly make
our way down that rock.

We stand in the line, waiting for the ferry to take us back.

Suddenly I turn to Jennifer. "Your father did it," I say.
"He hung himself."

Her expression doesn't change at all.

"He was in prison," I continue. "For drugs. And he
killed himself."

"I know," she says. "I found the death certificate last year
when we moved. I wanted my mother to tell me the truth."

I say, "That's the truth."

The ferry arrives, and we move forward, toward it. Its
steps are steep, and we have to link arms for the climb.

LOST PARTS

THE LAST THING Helen remembered before she missed the curve on Thurbers Avenue and sent her white Toyota Celica tumbling forty feet off the embankment until it finally settled roof-side down in a deserted lot, was looking at Scott in the passenger's seat beside her and saying, "What is wrong with you anyway?" She never got an answer. Instead, the car crashed, jumped, flew, landed. There were no screams or explosions, just the WGBH fund-raising drive, the fake intellectual accent of the classical music announcer asking for just ten more phone calls please. Scott, she was told later, died instantly of multiple head and neck injuries. Helen lost her spleen.

The spleen, a doctor explained, functions as a blood filter and as a place to store blood. He drew a picture in the air, plucking the invisible body part and tossing it, casually, Helen thought, over his shoulder. The doctor looked a little like Scott, and for a moment Helen considered asking him this hypothetical question: If you lived with your girlfriend for two years and suddenly you stopped getting along, fought over when the pasta was *al dente*, whether to watch

Letterman or *Nightline*, where to keep the unread magazines, would you start to sulk and sigh dramatically at odd
moments or would you break up or would you at least discuss what was wrong? But by the time the question was for-
mulated, he was already on his way out, his Nicole Miller tie,
decorated with hot pink stethoscopes and bright blue
syringes, flapping behind him.

Propped in her hospital bed, her stomach clamped shut
with staples, IVs in the tops of both hands, a slight Percocet
buzz in her head, Helen realized that after all the hours of
phone conversations with her friends, all the nights spent
awake staring down at Scott as he slept, all the daisies plucked
from their ridiculously small garden murmuring to herself,
"He loves me, he loves me not," after going to a palmist and a
tarot card reader—each with different opinions and predic-
tions—after all that, Helen realized she would never know
what Scott was thinking. Her question, "What is wrong with
you anyway?" would never be answered. Instead, it would
hang for eternity over the Thurbers Avenue curve.

HELEN'S FRIEND JOANNE knew the truth.

Helen had told her that she was going to break up with
Scott. I'll move out, Helen had said, and give us both some
breathing room.

So when Joanne appeared in Helen's hospital room,
dressed in black, she seemed embarrassed, red-faced with
downcast eyes.

She said, "God, your spleen. How awful." Even though
both of them knew that was not what was awful.

Helen answered by telling her about the staples.

Without looking at her, Joanne said, "My cousin's wife got really fat and had her stomach stapled so she couldn't eat a lot."

"I think those are internal staples," Helen said. "Mine are outside." Her hands fluttered above the damp gauze. A faint, strange smell came from the wound. A smell that Helen could not place. She supposed it was the smell of the insides of bodies. Scott, she'd been told, had no apparent injuries. No blood or gaping holes. Everything was internal; he looked fine.

"Did you see Scott?" Helen blurted.

Joanne looked up, frightened. Her mouth opened, then closed, then opened again.

"He . . . uh . . . died, Helen," she said. She indicated her black outfit as proof. Then she glanced into the hall for a nurse or someone to assist her.

Inappropriately, Helen laughed. "I know that," she said. "I meant . . ." She searched for the word. "Did you view him?"

Joanne lowered her voice, eased herself onto the very edge of Helen's hospital bed. "He looked great," she said.

They were silent, each contemplating, Helen supposed, what that meant. To Joanne, she supposed, it meant not dead. But to Helen it conjured images of Scott in his white boxer shorts, about to dress or undress, caught between things. That was when he looked vulnerable, open. Asleep, he kept his crotch guarded with both hands. Active, he was a frowner, a worrier, a man who disliked clutter, who complained she left her mail and necklaces and shopping lists in too many piles on every countertop.

"God," Helen said. "Dead."

She tried to think of what that meant. Really meant. If they had simply broken up, she would drink too much wine alone one night and call him, drunkenly, to cry. They would go to bed together a few more times, passionately. She would hate him, miss him, desire him. People would call her to say he had been spotted—at a café, in his car, mailing a letter. Dead was something else altogether.

She started to cry.

It wasn't the first time. The first time was when his parents arrived at her bedside, their faces red and blotchy, their eyes swollen, and told her they did not blame her. "That fucking curve," Scott's father had said. He was an economics professor at Brown and Helen had never heard him say "fuck" before. It startled her. Scott's mother said, "I know how much you loved him." That was when Helen began to cry. Did she? Love him? Hadn't she been thinking of breaking up with him? That very morning of the accident she had yelled at him for obsessively dust-busting around the litter box. "I am stepping on tiny pebbles!" he had shouted back at her.

Crying made her side ache and her staples itch. But once it started, there was nothing Helen could do.

"Hey," Joanne said, wrapping her arms awkwardly around Helen. "Come on."

"I killed Scott," Helen blabbered.

"No, you didn't," Joanne said, her voice soothing, the way a mother calms an infant.

But they both knew she had.

Helen could feel the impact, car against guardrail. She remembered being airborne, rocketing off the highway. In that instant, she had time-traveled back to her high school senior-class trip to Disney World, where she rode Space Mountain again and again, convinced dying felt like that.

Joanne was talking in that maternal voice, urging Helen to reconsider and spend the summer at an artists' colony in upstate New York with her. She had made that offer a few weeks ago. Joanne was a photographer; there would be other artists there. There would be cocktail parties. "I'll say you're my assistant," she'd said. "You can get away from Scott for a little while." But Helen had been unsure. Was getting away the right thing? Was a little while the right thing? Maybe they should be apart, she'd thought, forever.

Helen inhaled sharply, knowing it would hurt.

"It'll be fun," Joanne said, smiling sadly, squeezing Helen's hand.

"I think I will come," Helen said, her voice sounding slow and dreamlike. "But I don't think I could allow myself to have fun."

No one could look Helen in the eye. It was, she thought, as if they all knew something deep and dark about her, something horrifying. Even her own mother seemed to brighten when Helen told her she was going to spend the summer in upstate New York with Joanne. "Good for you," her mother said, cheerfully. Helen used to think Joanne's life was mysterious—artists! Scott worked in human resources at a bank; Helen taught composition at the junior college. When she'd told Joanne she was thinking about breaking up with Scott, Joanne had said, "I know a lot of interesting men." Helen had imagined black turtlenecks, clove cigarettes, thick coffee in little cups. She packed to go, avoiding Scott's drawers—the two top ones, his side of the closet. She pretended not to notice his *Newsweek*, so outdated now with Jackie Kennedy on the cover, folded open to the page where he'd left off the night before the accident. Scott would like that he died the same week as Jackie; it was the kind of thing he would have chosen. Helen's hands brushed against his glasses, ugly aviator-shaped ones that he wore only in the house, at night. The cold metal and glass made her recoil, step back. His other pair, his public ones, must have been in his suit pocket, she thought. For a crazy moment she considered packing the aviator glasses, taking them with her to New York. She imagined them nestled in her suitcase among her sweaters and socks and hiking boots. Her hand reached for them, sitting there on top of black and white pictures of a young, happy Jackie. But instead of picking them up, her hand hung there for a moment, suspended in midair, then dropped, heavily, to her side.

EVERYONE AT THE artists' colony assumed Joanne and Helen were lesbians.

A sculptor who "worked in wire" told Helen that every lesbian he knew wore shoes like hers.

A muralist named Ali told Helen that she had loved women at different times in her life. "When it was appropriate."

There was a nightly cocktail party followed by a slide show of one of the artists' work. The muralist painted familiar comic strip characters with their genitalia showing—Snoopy, Nancy, Cathy. Helen felt that she did not understand anything anyone was doing there. Everyone had come alone, except for a man named Andrew, who wouldn't tell her what he worked in. "That kind of question offends me," he said. Andrew had brought his children and a young nanny that everyone assumed he was sleeping with. His children were named Monday and Tuesday and were pasty skinned and sullen; the nanny, Danielle, was plump and cheerful, with honey-blond hair and bright eyes. Andrew, Helen decided, looked unclean. Like a man who didn't wash.

The slide show the first night was the work of a woman named Leila. Leila painted the names of body parts on wood along with their definition, function, and other meanings they might have. Helen was a little drunk by the time the slide show began, drunk in the way you can only get from too much sweet white wine and not enough food. She watched Leila's slides loom in front of her on the wall. LIVER, she read. A LARGE COMPOUND, TUBULAR, VERTEBRATE GLAND . . . The words jumped crazily and Helen had to close her eyes for an instant. ONE WHO LIVES IN A SPECIFIC MAN-NER, she read when she opened them again.

Then the slide changed abruptly and Helen was faced with a bigger than life definition of SPLEEN. She gasped. THIS ORGAN CONSIDERED AS THE SEAT OF MIRTH, MERRIMENT, CAPRICE.

"I lost my spleen," Helen whispered to the person next to her. In the dark, she could not make out who it was. She didn't even care. She was overwhelmed by guilt and some other unnameable emotion—grief, perhaps?

The person beside her leaned in so close to Helen that their shoulders touched. It was Danielle, the nanny. Helen felt Danielle's hair against her neck.

"Awesome," Danielle whispered back.

Foolishly, Helen grabbed Danielle's soft hand. It felt like freshly kneaded dough, begging Helen to press it, which she did, aggressively.

"Do you think that means I've lost my ability for happiness?" Helen asked her. She was no longer whispering. In fact, several people had turned around in their seats to glare.

Danielle remained unnerved. "I never knew," she said, keeping her own voice low, "that spleens were so expendable. Like an appendix. Or tonsils. I thought if you lost your spleen you'd die."

Helen was gulping air too quickly. Soon she would have the hiccups. That was what happened when she got nervous. She would get hiccups that nothing could stop—not holding her breath or being frightened or large spoonfuls of sugar.

"No," Helen managed to say. "You can die from multiple head injuries."

"Bummer," Danielle said.

She had not pulled away from Helen's desperate grip on her hand, and they now sat calmly, holding hands, Helen's hiccups beginning to escape.

The screen said: THYROID: OBSELETE DEFINITION: SHAPED LIKE A DOOR.

THAT NIGHT IN their little cabin, Joanne said to Helen, "Maybe it was a mistake, you coming here?"

Helen still had the hiccups. She was remembering how someone had once told her that a man in Scotland had the hiccups for thirteen years and then he finally killed himself.

"I mean," Joanne said, "why were you holding hands with the nanny?"

Helen couldn't think of a reasonable answer. "She has the softest hands in the world," she said finally.

Even though they were in the woods, it was noisy outside. People seemed to be running about, laughing loudly. Doors slammed. In the distance, Helen heard salsa music.

"I'm not sorry you came," Joanne said, which meant of course that she was, "but you have to respect people's work here."

"I do," Helen said quickly, afraid that Joanne was going to make her leave, send her back to the apartment in Providence, where Scott's clothes still hung in her closet, where the photograph of them sailing last summer—smiling, sunburned, arms thrown intimately around each other's bodies—would stare out at her as soon as she walked in.

"Leila is a very well respected artist," Joanne began.

Helen hiccuped loudly.

Joanne sighed, rolled over in her creaky cot.

The salsa music grew louder.

"I've got this strange urge to have a child," Helen said. "A baby."

Joanne didn't answer, but her bedsprings twanged some more, reminding Helen of the sad notes of a country-western song.

AT THE COCKTAIL party before the slide show the next night, Helen told Leila that her work had moved her immensely. Helen was afraid that everyone was going to gang up on her, force her to go. Joanne was right: she had to make more of an effort. Leila had pink skin and pale hair and the overall appearance of a rabbit. As Helen talked she was aware of her own nose twitching.

"Yes," Leila said to Helen, "I noticed you reacting."

Leila sounded like Greta Garbo. Everything about her was unnerving.

"Because," Helen said, pretending to have a bit of a cold so as to hide the twitching, "I lost my spleen in a tragic accident."

The words were true, but they seemed grandiose, embellished. But it had been tragic. Even now she could exactly recall the particular way the sunlight bounced through the windshield that morning, the smooth-shaven planes of Scott's face, his jaw chewing Dentyne fast. She remembered for the first time that he'd had two dots of blood from shaving on his neck. "Vampire bite," she'd said, poking him with two fingers.

"The spleen," Leila was telling her, "is a contradictory organ, don't you think? Merriment. Melancholy." She moved her hands like a scale to demonstrate.

"Melancholy?" Helen asked, trying not to twitch.

"You paid attention, no?" Leila said sharply.

"Yes, of course," Helen said. She downed her chablis and tried to find the table with the cheese log.

Had she missed something important? she wondered as she nibbled the sharp cheddar rolled in walnuts that she'd hastily smeared on a water cracker. Melancholy and merriment? Did that mean that she would lose all emotion now that she'd lost her spleen? She thought of Scott again. Before that inexplicable thing went wrong, they used to laugh together. It was what they'd had, she decided. What they'd lost. Merriment. Both of them could watch *Some Like It Hot* any time, any place. They played a word game that went like this: she'd say *center violin* and he'd say *middle fiddle. Bird ghost. Robin goblin. Northern tissue. Yankee hanky.* Helen started to cry.

That soft, doughy hand found hers again.

"I've been thinking about your spleen and stuff," Danielle said. "Once, when I was really bummed out, I dyed my hair red. It felt so good. Like, I was a redhead."

Helen looked at Danielle's honey-blond hair. It was straight and fine, parted in the middle, tucked behind her ears.

"There's this woman here? In town," Danielle continued. "Ashley? She does a good job. Everyone who comes up here at least gets highlights from her."

Helen's hand twisted a piece of her own brown hair. She had always liked that her hair was a good, solid medium brown. Not auburn or chestnut or mahogany.

"You don't have to go ballistic," Danielle told her. "But you'd be surprised."

"Ashley?" Helen said.

"Everyone goes to her." Danielle smiled. She had the sweet, innocent smile of a child.

The lights dimmed for the slide show. Helen sat down right where she was on the floor. Probably that would be considered disrespectful. But her side ached the way a person aches when they are homesick, or heartbroken.

HELEN KEPT WAKING up all night with the feeling that someone was holding her. Not holding her down or even tightly. She was just aware of arms around her waist, the sense of warm flesh, the weight of someone else. But of course when she woke up, she was alone. Joanne slept across the room. The salsa music played. People laughed. No one wrapped their arms around her. Helen settled back down in her small cot. But as she drifted back to sleep, the arms, the embrace, returned.

ON HER WAY to Ashley's—which was a short walk down a dirt road, past cows grazing, a broken fence, a pile of rocks, those were the directions she got—Helen practiced what she would say. I don't know why I'm doing this, she'd say. I like my hair. Nothing drastic, please. Nothing ballistic.

But then she saw the gently curving path that led to Ashley's log cabin and Helen, out of nowhere, imagined herself as a platinum blonde. Then with blue-black hair. She could even picture herself with *I Love Lucy* red. By the time she reached the front door, her heart was pounding. Inside this log cabin, she thought, was the power to change her.

The door opened before she knocked.

Ashley stood there, frowning, already studying the top of Helen's head. She was tall and thin, the kind of woman that Helen's mother called willowy. She had a powder puff of white-blond hair and round blue eyes. Her accent, when she finally spoke, was thick and southern.

"Lulabelle," she said to Helen, "your hair is earth and you are water. It is sapping you of nourishment, darling."

"Uh-huh," Helen said, and followed her inside.

Ashley turned to her. "I use no electricity, no chemicals, no toxins."

Helen swallowed hard. The cabin smelled like her old Lincoln Log set from when she was a child.

Ashley began massaging Helen's scalp. "Your hair is earth," she said again. "It gives life."

Helen gasped and moved away. "I killed Scott," she blurted.

As if she hadn't heard, Ashley's hands resumed their massaging. "It should be terra-cotta," she said finally. "And you need to drink more water. You are dehydrating from your soul outward."

She stopped massaging as abruptly as she began and left the room.

Helen's eyes had to adjust to the darkness—no electricity!—but when they did, she realized there was nothing much to see. The room, with its log walls and floors, was bare except for several chairs and an old-fashioned white porcelain basin. Helen supposed this was what it was like where Loretta Lynn grew up. She'd seen that movie about her life, the one with Sissy Spacek. That was a long time ago. Before she even knew Scott. Helen realized that Scott had not been in her life for most of her life. He had been with her for only three and a half years. When she had been thinking about breaking up with him, she'd come up with a theory that television shows outlive relationships. She'd had a boyfriend during the *Dynasty* years who was gone long before the show was canceled. Another that *L.A. Law* had outlived. She supposed had Scott not died, then he would have been her *Seinfeld* boyfriend. But he had died. Out of the blue. Without warning. So that now it would seem wrong, irreverent, to think of him in terms of *Seinfeld*. He was her dead boyfriend. He was the man she had accidentally killed. And it was wrong, irreverent, to think about how she'd been unhappy with him recently. His own grieving mother had told her they were so much in love. Helen could not tell her that wasn't true anymore. She thought again of those two dots of blood on his neck. Marking him. After she'd left the hospital and before she'd come to New York, Helen had gone to see Scott's parents. His father had talked about his neck. "It broke," he'd said, wringing his hands as if he were demonstrating how to kill a chicken. "It snapped."

Ashley stood there like a flamingo, long legs and arms bent at weird angles, balancing jars and pots of powders and creams on a tray.

"I don't want to go ballistic," Helen told her.

Ashley seemed to float toward her. Incense burned an unfamiliar, foreign smell.

"It's important, you think," Ashley said, easing Helen into a chair, "to maintain control."

Helen closed her eyes. "Yes," she said.

Ashley was mixing, rubbing, stroking, pouring water, applying hot, applying cold, wrapping, tugging.

Time slowed down, the way it had when Helen and Scott were in her car and it was airborne, flying off Thurbers Avenue. Was Scott already dead at that point? Helen wondered for the first time.

"Your hair tells me you should drive a Volvo," Ashley said.

"I recently totaled my Toyota," Helen told her.

"When your hair is terra-cotta and you drink more water, you will understand better." Ashley tapped her on the shoulders. "You can go now."

At a hair salon, a mirror hung in front of you, but here there were just logs.

Helen touched her hair, expecting it to feel different. But it didn't.

"You can leave your check in the mailbox at the end of the path," Ashley said. "I don't like to handle money so soon after I do someone's hair."

Helen felt let down somehow. "You don't have a . . . mirror?" she asked, though that wasn't what was really bothering her.

"In the back there's a pond with a fine reflection," Ashley said.

For a moment Helen thought she meant for her to go back there.

"But," Ashley continued, "I find no need to look at myself. At least, not my outer self."

"Right," Helen said.

On her way back, she imagined her hair was like a flower box cradling her head. That was what terra-cotta made her think of. Or Mexican pottery. Her hair was like a large jug. She tried to pull a piece in front of her so she could get a look, but it wasn't quite long enough.

Before she'd come up here, she'd gone for a haircut. Everyone in her salon back home knew what had happened—it had been the lead story on the six o'clock news the night of the accident—and acted strangely toward her, so strangely that Helen had felt frivolous for going in the first place, even though she'd worn a black turtleneck and asked for something "simple." As a result, she had a kind of shag that reminded her of a helmet.

The cocktail party was ending when she got back. Through the window, Helen saw people finding seats for the slide show, guzzling final glasses of wine before it was whisked away, settling in. She saw Joanne, with her head bent intimately toward the sculptor who worked in wire. Helen slipped in the back door and took a seat in the last row. Joanne was flirting with that man. Hadn't they both giggled at his phrase "worked in wire"? It sounded painful, they'd laughed. Now Joanne was—stroking his thigh! During the day, the artists supposedly went into their little private studios and worked. Lunch was delivered silently, anonymously, on their doorsteps in solemn brown bags. When did Joanne have time to get to the point where she would stroke this guy's inner thigh?

"Rocks," a woman's voice said.

The slide showed dozens of rocks, all flat and smooth.

"They do not betray us," the voice continued.

The slide changed.

A black rock with white writing appeared on the wall. MURDERER.

Next slide.

BIRTH.

Then the lights went on.

Joanne and the wire man were gone! Helen looked around the room frantically. They had slipped out. They were in his cabin, Helen realized, fucking. She was trembling. A woman came up to her, took a rock from a pail, and handed it to her with a piece of colored chalk. Pink.

"On one side," the voice said, "write the word that describes the best side of you. On the other side, the worst."

Some people began to scribble right away. Others thought first, then wrote more carefully. But Helen just stared at her blank rock. She remembered how as a child she would collect rocks on the beach, glue them together, and paint the words ROCK CONCERT on them. She gave them as Christmas presents.

"You went," Danielle said. Her rock had bright blue writing on it.

Helen nodded.

"Did it help?" Danielle said.

She looked so hopeful that Helen smiled and nodded.

Helen wished she could read what Danielle had written on her rock. She wished she could read all the rocks. But she supposed that was like reading someone else's mail. Unethical.

Danielle was bending down to be closer to Helen. She said, "This guy I went to high school with? Jerry? He got shot in a hunting accident and they had to cut off his leg."

Helen pulled away. Was this what she had become? Someone to tell horrible stories to?

But Danielle moved closer again. "And this guy, Jerry, said that at night his leg would itch. The leg that wasn't there! It would itch! Or cramp!"

Helen had heard of this phenomenon before. She'd heard that women who'd lost their babies still heard them cry at night.

"A phantom limb," Helen said.

"What I wonder is if you still feel your spleen," Danielle said.

"Oh," Helen said, relaxing, "well, no. I mean, I never really felt it in the first place, when it was there."

Danielle considered that. "Wow," she said at last.

In the cabin, Helen finally saw her hair. It did not look very different, though she examined it closely. She separated large pieces of it, let them fall slowly back into place. She made a cat's cradle of hair with her fingers, searching for the change, the claylike color. It seemed shinier, perhaps. It felt softer. She smelled, vaguely, salad smells coming from it. She wished Joanne would come back so she could get a second opinion. But Joanne was with the wire man, fondling him. Being fondled.

Helen got into bed and closed her eyes.

There was no salsa music tonight. In fact, it was quiet. Everyone had probably paired off. Everyone was making love. She found that she could not remember the feel of Scott's kisses or touches or what exactly it was like in the instant when he entered her, before movement began. She had forgotten. No. She could almost remember the way his hand felt resting on her leg when they slept, the light weight of it, flesh on flesh.

At some point in the night, she woke herself, sat upright in her bed, said out loud, "What is wrong with you anyway?" felt her heartbeat quicken as if an answer might really come, as if she would feel a crash, go airborne, know something more. But she sat like that, waiting, until she fixed herself in that place, that cabin, that cot, alone.

AT FIRST, HELEN thought she was dreaming, that it was still night and she was asleep. But slowly she came to realize that someone really was in the cabin touching her forehead with their fingertips.

"Hi," Danielle said when Helen opened her eyes. "That's how I like to wake up. By someone writing me messages on my head."

Danielle had on some kind of white lace bonnet and looked vaguely Amish.

Helen's mouth was cottony.

"You were writing me messages on my head?" she said.

"Just like 'Hi' and 'Ellen' and stuff," Danielle giggled.

By the cast of the sunlight streaming through the window, Helen realized it was already afternoon.

"My name is Helen. Not Ellen," she said, struggling to sit up. Her side throbbed.

"Really?" Danielle said, surprised. "I thought Helen was an old person's name. But I know a lot of young Ellens."

Helen got up and went to look at her terra-cotta hair in the light. Besides being flat from too much sleep, her hair looked the same.

"I've got a confession to make," Danielle said.

Helen realized she had missed both breakfast and lunch. She looked at Joanne's unslept-in bed, then out the window where, in those woods, the studios sat. If Joanne was still with the sculptor, maybe Helen could go and steal her brown bag lunch.

"Remember that guy Jerry I told you about?" Danielle was asking.

"The phantom limb?"

"Cool," Danielle said. "You're a good listener." She pointed at Helen happily.

"What about him?" Helen wanted Danielle to leave. The bonnet was bothering her. Danielle was bothering her.

"I did it," Danielle said. "I shot him."

Helen took a step backward. "It wasn't a hunting accident?" She had seen made-for-TV movies about crazy women who stalked men and shot them. She had seen *Fatal Attraction*.

"It was a hunting accident," Danielle said. "I thought he was a wild turkey, you know? It was right before Thanksgiving and we were turkey hunting and I shot him."

Knowing that Danielle wasn't deranged, Helen wondered why she didn't feel more relieved.

"He was my boyfriend," Danielle added. "Then I felt really guilty for breaking up with him because he, like, only had one leg and stuff. What a nightmare. Anyway, I decided not to hide it anymore. I shot him and he lost a leg and then I broke up with him, and maybe that makes me a bad person, but that is what happened." She exhaled loudly. "I feel better telling you the truth."

They stood looking at each other across a shaft of sunlight filled with dancing dust motes until Danielle remembered that she was supposed to take Monday and Tuesday swimming.

That was when Helen saw that the Amish bonnet was actually a bathing cap.

On her way to steal Joanne's lunch, Helen tried to figure out why she hadn't told Danielle about Scott. It was the same kind of situation, in a way. Except Scott had died and they hadn't gotten the chance to break up and this guy Jerry lost a leg and got his heart broken. Was one worse? Helen wondered.

Joanne's lunch was already gone, which meant she was probably inside her studio.

Helen peeked in the window.

There was Joanne, not working, the brown bag empty, crumpled.

She saw Helen looking at her and waved.

"You know," Helen said, "people end up in a lot of unusual situations. It doesn't make them bad."

Joanne frowned.

"I can't believe you fucked the wire man," Helen said.

"His work is very sensitive," Joanne said, sounding haughty. "He spins it. Like cotton candy."

It was Helen's turn to frown.

"It might do you some good to make contact with another man," Joanne said.

Helen felt like an alien. Make contact. Take me to your leader.

"Who?" Helen said. "Andrew?"

Joanne ignored her. "I thought you were getting your hair colored."

"I did," Helen said. "Terra-cotta."

Joanne shrugged.

Beside the bag was an apple core and cookie crumbs.

"It cost seventy-five dollars and it looks exactly the same," Helen said.

"Actually," Joanne said thoughtfully, "it looks worse."

"What do you expect?" Ashley said. "You didn't do what I told you."

"What?" Helen said, waving her arms. "Buy a Volvo?"

Ashley bent down and returned to her gardening. She had splotches of dirt all over her bare arms and legs and sweat marks on her tee shirt. Her hair was the exact color of the carrots she pulled from the dirt.

"I needed help," Helen said. Her voice was coming from somewhere deep inside of her. It was rising up out of her. It was erupting. "I came to you for help."

Ashley's garden bursted with vegetables. Everywhere Helen looked, something was growing, sprouting, budding.

Ashley pointed her hoe at Helen. "You said you didn't want anything drastic."

"But I wanted something Now I have nothing. I'm worse off than before."

It was too hot out there in Ashley's garden, and the air was heavy with the smell of dirt, of the earth. Helen thought she might choke or faint. Without thinking about it, Helen dropped to her knees, right into the dirt, and sobbed. She thought she might die, right there.

"You are losing control," Ashley said.

Helen clutched at the earth, began to dig. Her hands hit something hard. Radishes. Small, perfect, red ones.

"Do not ruin my garden," Ashley said. She dropped her hoe and made her way toward the log cabin.

Helen got to her feet, shaky, uncertain. She could not stop crying. She held on to her little bunch of radishes and made her way back toward her own cabin.

Somehow—the sun?—Helen wandered the wrong way through the woods. She missed the broken fence, the pile of stones, the grazing cows, and ended up by the studios.

There was Joanne's.

Helen went to the window. Joanne was in there, with the wire man. They were clothed, sitting across from each other. But when Joanne glanced up and saw Helen standing there, she looked away, guilty.

Disoriented, Helen made yet another wrong turn. The smell of dirt clung to her, confused her.

At the next studio, Helen hesitated. There was a strict

rule about disturbing the artists during work time. She felt relieved when the door opened and one of the artists stepped out. Although he looked familiar, she could not remember who he was exactly. The potter? The abstract expressionist?

"Helen?" he said. "Is that right?"

She went to shake his hand, but it looked like she was offering him the radishes.

He laughed. "Radishes," he said. Then he took them.

"Actually," Helen said, "I sort of stole those."

Carefully, he wiped each radish on his shirt. "Then we'd better eat them. Destroy the evidence."

He held one out to her. There was color on his hands. Terra-cotta, Helen thought.

They ate the radishes in silence, except for the crunching.

Helen wanted to tell him something, but she could not form the words.

HELEN TOOK HER blank rock and the piece of pink chalk from her desk drawer. She sat cross-legged on her bed.

Joanne had told her that she and the wire man might be falling in love.

She said it like a confession.

"It's okay," Helen had told her.

"I like this part," Joanne said, "when you think the very things that will later drive you crazy, maybe even drive you apart, are quirky and wonderful. When everything you do or say, they find fascinating."

"This is the happy part," Helen said.

"Right," Joanne said. "Then you get used to each other, maybe even move in together, maybe even get married, and the laundry doesn't get done and he hates your friends and you get sick of going to obscure foreign movies with him and you can't remember the last time the two of you took a shower together."

"The real part," Helen said.

"Right. Then maybe you realize you've fallen out of love and it's over."

Helen felt something strange where her spleen used to be. She realized it no longer hurt very much. The itching had stopped.

"The sad part," Helen said.

"Or," Joanne had said, smiling, stretching in that slow, catlike way that people who are having a lot of good sex do, "love wins out."

Helen smoothed her already smooth rock.

On one side, she wrote MERRIMENT.

On the other, she wrote MELANCHOLY.

She put the rock back in the drawer.

ON THE DAY before they went back home, Helen made her way to Ashley's log cabin again. There were the cows, the fence. But the pile of stones was gone. Helen wondered if the woman rock artist—she and Joanne called her Wilma—had stolen them.

Ashley was in her garden again, though not gardening. She was sitting there, bent like a piece of origami.

Helen stood in front of her, waiting.

Finally Ashley opened her eyes.

"You," she said.

"I took some radishes," Helen told her. "That day."

Ashley nodded and unfolded herself. "If you want, I'll do your hair again. For half price.

But Helen didn't want her hair colored. "I just wanted to tell you about the radishes."

"Can I ask you something?" Ashley said.

"What?"

"Who's Scott?"

Helen narrowed her eyes. "How do you know about Scott?"

"You told me when I did your hair. You said, 'I killed Scott.'"

Helen was surprised to see that a few leaves at the very top of a maple tree had already turned to scarlet. Those leaves made her—almost—happy.

"He was my boyfriend," Helen told Ashley. "He died in an accident."

"The Toyota," Ashley said.

Helen saw that today Ashley's hair was, oddly, the color Scott's had been. A rich brown, the color of wet dirt.

"We were on the very verge of breaking up when it happened," Helen added.

She looked from Ashley to the tall stalks of corn behind her, to the woods that stretched beyond them. If she walked through those woods she would reach Vermont, then Massachusetts, and then, finally, home. Standing there in the fading sunlight, Helen could imagine that, could imagine walking and walking until she found her way back.

DROPPING BOMBS

JIM TOLD HIS mother everything. He explained every detail, every reason, every step. How Aunt Dodie could drive her to the airport and wait with her while she picked up her ticket. How to pack in a small bag that she could take on the plane with her so she wouldn't have to worry about her things getting lost. How once she boarded, she did not have to worry about anything at all because the pilot would do the rest. "Once you take off," he told her, "just sit back and relax." He even sent her some paperbacks and a stack of cooking magazines to read en route. "You'll be in Los Angeles in time for lunch," he said.

But still she couldn't handle it. With increased airport security he couldn't meet her at the gate, so Jim told her to wait for him at baggage claim. "But you said not to check a bag," Eve said, and Jim could hear the shrill panic rising in her voice. "Just follow the signs to baggage claim. Hell," he told her, "follow all the other passengers. Then just stand there. I'll find you." Instead, she stood at the gate, frozen there in her new mauve pantsuit, clutching her bag to her chest, eyes wild like a trapped animal.

Jim got to the airport almost an hour early and stood watching each new planeload of passengers arrive and claim their bags. Even after everyone left, the luggage carousels kept spinning, sending a few unclaimed bags around again and again. Jim kept wondering who owned those bags. Wasn't that unsafe? Couldn't some crazed terrorist check a bag with a bomb in it and then not board the flight at all? Those bags worried him, circling endlessly like that.

A redcap passed him.

"Excuse me," Jim said, and he pointed toward Carousel C. The same two bags had been going around on it since Jim arrived, a small brown leather one that looked like a mail pouch and a beat-up, dusty blue duffel bag.

The redcap looked at Jim like he didn't trust him. The whites of his eyes were yellow. They reminded Jim of eggs.

"Those bags," Jim said, wagging his finger,"whose are they?" Slowly, the man turned and studied the circling luggage.

"Well," he said, "how am I supposed to know that now?" He pointed too, at Carousel B, where a fresh group of passengers jockeyed for position. "Whose bags are those?" he said, and he wagged his finger at the luggage cluttering the carousel. "You think I go around, matching up bags with people?"

The man wore his hat far back on his head, revealing a short, military-type haircut. For an instant, Jim pictured him fighting a war, in Korea maybe, rushing forward, angry and mean.

"You think I got nothing better to do?" the man was saying.

"It just seems dangerous," Jim said. "That's all." He was aware that he was still half-pointing, his wrist drooping slightly, his finger pointing downward.

"Yeah," the redcap said. "Them bags are real dangerous. You keep your eye on them."

He lifted his empty cart, aiming toward Carousel B, where passengers were claiming their luggage now in a frenzy that reminded Jim of animals gobbling their prey on *National Geographic* specials.

A loudspeaker crackled and a voice announced, "James Morgan, please meet your mother at the TWA ticket counter, upper level."

"Shit," Jim said, startled to hear his own name like that.

The redcap had started to move away from him. As he wheeled past Jim he muttered, "Faggot."

"I can't believe you didn't come for me. I waited just like you said. I waited and waited. Finally this nice girl, maybe a stewardess, I don't know, she came up to me and said, 'Are you lost?' and I told her my son was supposed to be there. That he was late or forgot or something." Eve glared at him. "I waited forever, just like you said."

They were at an outdoor restaurant in Venice, eating lunch. His mother had told Jim the story twice already, first when he claimed her and then again in the car on their way here. She also told him it was impossible to read on the flight. "You have to stay alert," she said. "Anyone could be a hijacker. A Shiite Moslem or Libyan terrorist. Who knows? Do you think Klinghoffer, cruising like that on the Mediterranean, expected to be shot and dumped in the sea? You don't know who to trust." She'd handed him the paperbacks and cooking magazines, still in the padded shipping envelope he'd sent them in.

Now Jim pointed toward the parade of people that whizzed past them on rollerblades, bicycles, skateboards, and rollerskates. "Look at them," he told his mother. "See how everyone looks different out here."

She snorted. "So I noticed," she said. "Too many of them dye their hair. And they spend too much time in the sun. Don't they read out here? It's very dangerous." She sipped her iced tea and made a face. "This is terrible."

"I mean they're more active," Jim said. "Health conscious. Any day of the week you'll see people out here like this."

"Great," Eve said. "Wonderful." She looked around until she spotted their waiter, then motioned him over. "What is in this tea?" she said to him.

He was handsome, tanned and blond with a dimple in his chin. He looked first at Jim and smiled, then at Eve. "Fresh mint," he said. "Isn't it yummy?"

"If I wanted mint," she said, "I'd chew gum."

The waiter looked at Jim again. Jim felt a warm familiar rush in his gut. Sometimes he wondered if the real reason he had moved to L.A. was because he liked these surfer boys so much. He imagined for an instant this waiter naked, no tan lines, a smooth hairless chest.

"Could I just have some water?" Eve was saying.

"You bet," the waiter said, smiling again. When he left, he brushed against Jim, so lightly it felt like the breeze from the water that lay ahead of them.

Eve studied Jim's face, hard.

"What?" he said.

She shook her head.

Jim cleared his throat and looked off toward the ocean. He had lived in L.A. for almost three years and this was the first time his mother had come to visit. He'd asked her in the past, tried to lure her here with promised trips to Mann's Chinese Theatre and Disneyland, places that she'd always heard about and thought she'd never see. Secretly, he was always relieved when she refused to come. She would say, "I'll see you out here at Christmas anyway. Right?" And he would feel a ballooning in his chest, a fullness that he liked. He would think, Good. It was like buying a few more months of not having to tell her.

Once, she'd said yes, then canceled at the last minute. "There are some things I really don't want to see," she'd said as way of an explanation. That had startled Jim. What exactly had that meant? Even now he wondered if she was trying to tell him something, if maybe she knew somehow already. But that seemed impossible. When he'd lived in Chicago, just an hour from her house in the suburbs, he was still pretending, even to himself. He used to date girls who were pretty, former Homecoming queens, girls who dressed in pale colors, who wore soft fuzzy sweaters and pink lipstick. Last Christmas he noticed that his mother still had a picture of him with one of those girls, one she especially liked named Debbie, right on top of the television set. In it, Jim is slightly behind Debbie, so that it is her smiling, heart-shaped face that dominates. It is her locket, her wispy blond bangs and bright pink lips that you noticed. Jim was really in the background, a blur.

"Jim?" his mother said. She reached across the table and squeezed his hand. "Jim," she said again, "how are you? Are you happy?"

He had decided that if she really came this time, he would tell her. But now he wasn't so sure. She did not seem ready. Why, even a glass of tea with mint in it threw her into a tizzy! Even the sight of healthy, tanned people upset her! Sometimes, when he was alone, her face floated in front of him, frowning and disappointed, holding all the pain of knowing the truth, of knowing there would never be a big church wedding at Our Lady of Perpetual Sorrow, or grand-children, or even him at home for Christmas with his lover beside him. Right now, his mother's face seemed open, expectant even, as if she were waiting for him to say it. He wondered again if she already knew.

"I . . ." he began. He felt his hand beginning to sweat beneath hers.

"What?" she said. She leaned toward him. "What?"

His throat felt dry, scratchy. "I am," he said.

The pressure on his hand increased.

"You are what, Jim?" she said.

Her eyes were wet. Maybe from the salt air, Jim thought. He said, "Yes. I am happy."

Eve's hand slipped off his, and settled back into her lap. There were circles of sweat under the arms of her mauve jacket. On the pocket she wore a rhinestone pin of an owl with glittering green eyes.

Suddenly the waiter was back with her water. He placed it in front of her with a flourish, then winked at Jim. Jim realized his heart was pounding, but he wasn't sure if it was from how close he had come to finally telling her the truth, or from the closeness of this blond man whose nametag read RANDY.

"Thanks, Randy," Jim said, pronouncing the name with great care.

"Ugh," Eve said, spitting water back into the glass. "What's in here?"

Randy's face clouded. "Lemon," he said.

Eve slumped back into her seat, defeated.

"Maybe we could just take the check?" Jim said.

Randy nodded. When he returned with it, he slipped Jim a note written on a napkin. Their eyes met for just an instant. Jim's hands shook slightly as he read the note: "Call me?" and Randy's name and phone number. Jim looked up. His mother was staring at him. He glanced away from her, his eyes seeking out Randy. He saw him, across the patio, waiting. Jim gave him the slightest nod.

"Ready?" he said to his mother.

"What's on that napkin?" she said.

The sun had shifted and seemed to be boring right through Jim's skull. It made him slightly light-headed. He shrugged.

Eve frowned at him. "I waited forever," she said.

"No, you didn't," he told her. "You were in the wrong place. I was right where I was supposed to be."

"No," she said. "You weren't."

EVE WAS SUPPOSED to stay for five days. But after three she told Jim she wanted to go home. "I don't like it here," she said. "A person can't even get a drink of water that tastes right. You can't walk anywhere. Always in the car. Drive, drive, drive. And everything seems wrong, smaller or something." She was disappointed in the stars' homes he drove her past, disappointed in the Hollywood sign, disappointed in the Ramos gin fizzes at the Beverly Hills Hotel. They saw Mel Gibson in a restaurant and she was disappointed in him too. "Even he's smaller than he seems," she said. Jim was afraid she was going to cry.

On the night she announced she was leaving on a flight the next day, Jim said, "Then we'll go out somewhere special for dinner."

But Eve shook her head. "We haven't spent any time together."

"Ma," he said, "we've been together constantly for three straight days."

"Not really. You've been keeping me busy all the time. So we don't have to talk."

"Don't be ridiculous," Jim said.

"Remember when your father left?" his mother asked him. Eve patted the couch beside her. Reluctantly, Jim went and sat there. She had on the mauve pantsuit again. Jim caught a slightly sour smell coming from her. "He sent us up to the lakehouse for a weekend and when we got back he had moved out."

"I remember," Jim said. He remembered how hot it was that night, how the crickets seemed to sing extra loud, cracking through the summer air. They had walked inside and found most of the furniture gone, the refrigerator empty, and a note. His mother had sat down on the yellow and green linoleum and sobbed. Jim was seven.

"In some ways," Eve said now, "you're like him."

"Thanks a lot," Jim said. "That's a real compliment. Especially knowing how you feel about him."

Instead of getting angry, his mother smiled at him, a small, sad smile.

"I'm not like him," Jim said. He had not seen his father in over ten years. Once, his father had taken him camping. To

Jim, that was the last time they were together, although his mother told him he was wrong. Jim had refused to go to the bathroom in the woods and his father had yelled at him, taken him home early. "You disgust me," his father told him in the car. When they got to his mother's, Jim ran out of the car and up the walk. "You run like a girl," his father shouted after him.

"I said in some ways," Eve said. "The way you avoid talking about things, for example."

"Fine. I'll talk," Jim said too loudly. He jumped off the couch and stood before her, fists and jaw clenched. "What do you want to know?"

"Well," she said, "for instance, are you dating anyone special?"

"No," he said. That was the truth. He had been dating a man whose name, strangely, was also Jim. But they had broken up a few months back and the man had moved to Tucson.

"Are you dating anyone at all?" she said.

"Yes," Jim said, truthfully again. Last night, after his mother went to sleep, he had called Randy, the waiter, from the phone in his bedroom. They had talked for an hour and set up a date for Monday night. Jim was going to cook him dinner here.

"Who?"

"What is this?" Jim said. He recognized the shrillness in his voice. It was just like hers. "Even if I tell you, you won't know them. You don't know anyone here except for me, do you?"

Eve didn't say anything. She just sat there, waiting. Wasn't this what he'd brought her here for? To tell her? But Jim could not think of what to say exactly, or how to say it.

Finally he said, "Can we go to dinner now?" He felt exhausted. He felt like he could sleep for days without waking up. He imagined doing just that, crawling into bed and going to sleep. When he finally woke up, she would be gone, back in her own house with Debbie's picture smiling out at her, comforting her.

"Are you still a good cook?" Eve said, her voice soft.

"Yes."

"Cook me dinner then. It's our last night."

HE GRILLED CHICKEN coated with Dijon mustard, and potatoes. He tossed a big salad. They sat outside on his small patio to eat. Eve admired his garden, the lush tomatoes and baby lettuce. Jim drank too much wine on purpose.

"You know what's a shame?" his mother said. "That I have to fly back. I'm terrified."

"It's safer than driving in a car," he told her. He had told her that before she came too.

"I don't believe that."

"Well, it's true," he said, trying not to sound irritated.

"Don't believe everything you hear," she said. "How do you think those people felt when that bomb went off and they fell out of the sky?"

"What people?"

"All those people on that Pan Am jet. Flight 103. And right before Christmas. I saw all those mothers on TV who had lost children." She took a big breath. "There is nothing worse than losing your child. Nothing."

Drunkenly, Jim threw his arm around his mother's shoulders and placed a too-wet kiss on her cheek. "Well," he said, "you're stuck with me no matter what."

She laughed. "Stuck," she said. "Hardly. You're the one stuck with me."

The image of those unclaimed bags, circling, suddenly popped into Jim's mind again. He frowned, and the arm he'd tossed so casually around his mother tightened into a hug.

"Don't worry," he said. "No one wants to bomb a plane to Chicago."

She hugged him back, hard. "Oh, Jim," she said, "you're wrong. Bombs fall all the time. Unexpected. If people knew when they were going to drop, they'd avoid them, avoid getting hurt. Those people on that Pan Am plane, you think they would have gotten on had they known?"

"I don't know," he said. He held his mother at arm's length. She seemed ready for anything. But hadn't she just told him that a person wouldn't walk into a situation where a bomb was going to drop? He got up and moved toward the door that led inside.

"Where are you going?" Eve said.

He smiled at her, happy that she was sitting here on his patio at dusk, happy that tomorrow she would be gone.

"Dessert," he said. "The grand finale." And he went inside to get it, vanilla ice cream with cherries. He would come back out, pour cherry liqueur on top, then hold a match to it until, right before their eyes, it burst into flames.

"SO," JIM SAID as they stood together at the airport waiting for his mother's flight to board, "Aunt Dodie will pick you up? She'll be there waiting?"

Eve nodded. She had on a different pantsuit, a lemon yellow one with a pin of a clown on the lapel. Despite the bright color, the cheerful pin, she looked older, worried. Even when she smiled up at him, her frown did not disappear completely.

Jim watched a young couple kissing goodbye. The girl seemed hungry, starved even. His mother turned and watched too, as the boy kneaded the girl's rear end, pushing her into him greedily.

"Young love," Eve said, and turned away. Her frown deepened.

Jim could not take his eyes from them, from the curve of the girl's neck as she tilted her head, from the boy's slender fingers pressing her flesh. He wore a Yankees baseball hat, she wore floral leggings.

"Jim," his mother told him, "don't stare."

But he continued to watch. What would become of them? he wondered. They would grow up, fall out of love, never feel this way again. Or they would get married and grow to hate each other, forget this day when they could not bear to say goodbye. Maybe he would board this plane and it would get blown up. Maybe he carried the bomb himself.

"You're being rude," Eve said.

Jim sighed and turned away from the couple. His mother seemed to have shrunk in these few minutes since he last looked at her. She looked old, frail.

"Oh," she said, "I hate to fly. I'll never come to see you again, unless you move closer to home."

"I won't," he told her softly.

She looked out the window, at a plane taxiing in. "If you fall out of a plane at thirty-five thousand feet, you vaporize," she said distractedly. "Zap! Gone. Just like that."

"Well, then, you'd better keep your seat belt fastened,"

he said. In that moment he decided he could not tell her. Not now, not ever. She was unable to handle it. She worried about sun exposure, vaporizing, bombs, and hijacking. At her own house, he knew, she had installed an elaborate alarm system. His mother was afraid to fly, afraid of everything. He saw again Debbie's face smiling out from on top of the television.

Eve tugged at his arm. "They're calling my flight now."

"I wish . . ." he said, but didn't finish.

"I wish you could come with me, see me on the plane safely." She took her bag from him. "Will you wait here and watch until I've taken off safely? That way if the plane goes down, you'll be right here."

Jim had no intention of doing anything so ridiculous but he said, solemnly, "Yes. I'll wait right here." He kissed her quickly on the cheek. "Have a good trip. Have a Bloody Mary or something. Relax."

She began to move away from him, toward security. "Ha!" she said. "Easy for you to say. You'll have your feet planted firmly on the ground."

Jim waved goodbye. He turned, and the couple was gone, vanished, like they were never there at all.

Suddenly, his mother was back, standing right in front of him, her face close to his. "Jim," she said, "I think it's a shame that people can't be who they are. Whatever that is. If someone loves you, they don't care what you are. They love you no matter what. You have to be yourself. Be happy with who you are." She reached up and held his face in her hands. "There is nothing worse than losing a child. That's what they say. You're my only child, my boy. And I love you. I accept you for what you are. Do you know that?"

He nodded. He tried to speak but she was off again, walking away from him with great determination, like a small, lemon yellow soldier.

"Mom," he called after her. "Thank you."

She didn't look back. She just lifted her arm and waved, then disappeared down the long hall to her gate.

Slowly, Jim began to walk away. She had left two days early so he still had time off from work. He thought of calling Randy and asking him if he wanted to drive up to Big Sur for a few days. Yes, he thought, he would go home and do that. The loud roar of a jet engine revving made him stop. That would be his mother's plane, carrying her back home.

He turned and went back to the big window that looked out over the runway. Jim pressed his palms against the glass. His breath steamed a small O in front of him. The plane moved slowly down the runway, then picked up speed, and began to take off. Jim's heart beat hard against his chest as he watched. He realized he was holding his breath. Then the plane soared into the sky, lifting higher and higher, taking his mother upward, and away. Jim stood like that, palms pressed against the cool, smooth glass, eyes following the now speck of a plane, until he could no longer see it, and he was sure his mother would not fall from the sky.

INSIDE

GORBACHEV'S HEAD

ELLIOT IS WAITING on Angell Street for the woman he loves. She is Georgia, his mother's friend. At 8:20 he finally sees her. She's driving a BMW 2002, Amazon green and rickety, and stalls right in front of his dorm, where he's been standing and waiting for fifteen cold, gray, early morning minutes. Instead of getting the car started again, she leans across the seats and opens the passenger door from the inside.

"Get in, Elliot," Georgia says. "I can't be late for my shrink."

Everybody his mother knows, his mother included, has a shrink; Elliot believes there is an entire population of women over forty getting analyzed, Prozaced, and twelve stepped to death.

He can't get the door shut and Georgia can't get the car started, so they both sit there with their private struggles until finally the car turns over and Georgia says, "Hold the door shut if you have to." There's no seat belt. The door rattles. It's a precarious situation. Still, Elliot manages to notice what Georgia's wearing—black leggings, brown Doc Martens boots, a thick woolen sweater, probably Guatemalan, with abstract people dancing across the lumpy wool and too many loose threads.

Georgia lights up a cigarette and offers him one.

Even though he wants to take it, he shakes his head, afraid of balancing the cig and a match without falling out of the car, which is now darting through Providence like an amusement park ride.

"I thought smoking was back," Georgia says. "I can't keep up anymore." She wraps her full lips around her cigarette and inhales, deeply. Her lipstick makes him think of seaweed, wet and dark, and that makes him think of sex, so he tries to push other images into his mind—Miró's Nocturnals, the '86 World Series—but it's too late. He's sitting in Georgia's car and he can see her calf muscles push against her leggings when she brakes. Every time Elliot is around Georgia he thinks like this. He tries the direct approach and looks right at her, blatantly. Even lustfully, he thinks. Her hair is dyed an unnatural black and falls in tight springs around her face and down her shoulders. He imagines her pubic hair, where it begins and how it must be wild and untamed. Her voice makes him think of a smoky bar.

"What?" she says when she catches him staring, but he just shrugs and tries to stop imagining her naked.

She pops in a tape, Counting Crows, and keeps smoking. Her eyes are hidden behind crooked Wayfarers, but Elliot knows they are dark brown, deep set, lined in black. He has known Georgia since he was seven and she lived in Manhattan, on Bank Street, in a fifth-floor walk-up that looked the way he has come to think apartments in Paris must look. Whenever he thinks of that apartment it seems there were constants—sheer curtains always moved in the breeze, fresh flowers sat in bowls, the espresso machine gurgled. There was always sunlight, somewhere.

They used to visit her, Elliot and his mother, every Saturday, from their oversized Colonial in Chappaqua, forty minutes by train. Georgia had three cats, Abyssinians, and cat hair all over her clothes and couch. She always had a disaster—a broken heart, unrequited love, or the wrong man pursuing her. Once, a former boyfriend even stalked her and she lived, or so she told them, in fear for months. His mother would listen; she would nurse Georgia's frequent hangovers; they would all three go for a walk; Georgia would nod and smoke and not take any of his mother's advice. Back home in Chappaqua his mother made him take a hot bath right away. While she did the laundry she mumbled, about germs and cats and Georgia.

"Providence is such a hole," Elliot blurts above the BMW's noisy muffler. Having thought of Georgia on Bank Street, it almost hurts to think of her anywhere else. "How can you stand it?"

Georgia shrugs. "It's not so bad," she says.

But it is. Everyone keeps reminding Elliot how lucky he is to be here, at Brown, but he misses the lawns and trees of home, the order that prevails there. Georgia is here because she teaches at RISD, but mostly she is an artist; she paints in thick, dark oils. Her paintings are always described as masculine, but Elliot doesn't agree. They are big, intimidating, earthy, like Georgia herself. Once, in her bathroom on Bank Street, he took her pantyhose that were hanging over the shower to dry and sniffed them, the feet and crotch and long leg part in between. Under the smell of Dove soap, he caught a vague whiff of Georgia. Remembering it, he leans toward her to try to find it again. But all he smells is stale smoke and old leather.

They are already at the cutoff for the airport.

"This state is so small you can't even get lost," Elliot mumbles.

"Have you been to the Indian place?" Georgia asks. "We should do Indian when you get back."

That is not the way to talk to your friend's kid, but Georgia has no experience. She did have her own kid, but she gave it up for adoption and then moved to Mexico. Elliot knows all her secrets from the days when he used to go with his mother to visit her. That kid would be his own age, twenty. A boy. "I didn't even hold him," Georgia told his mother on one of those long-ago Saturdays. She did not sound sad. "I handed him over and headed south." Briefly, Elliot wonders what became of him, Georgia's son. Maybe he's like me, he thinks. Maybe he's even at Brown. Maybe he and Georgia pass each other on Waterman Street every day.

"It's bring-your-own," Georgia is saying, still talking about the Indian restaurant.

"Whatever," he says. Georgia and Elliot have lived seven blocks from each other all semester and this is the first time he's seen her.

Georgia leans close to him. "Give your mother a big kiss for me, okay?"

He smells it. *Her* smell. He's afraid he's actually drooling. Does he even mumble, "Thanks," as he lurches out of the car? She sits there, stalled, trying to turn it over for as long as it takes him to check his bag and get a boarding pass.

On his way to the coffee shop, Elliot walks past the big plate-glass window, conspicuous. He wonders if he should do something to help, but he can't for the life of him think what that might be.

IN THE THREE months since Elliot was last home, his mother has married their next-door neighbor, Mr. Rickey, and gotten knocked up. Elliot doesn't know what to expect when the Westchester Airport Service drops him off at the house. It looks the same, at least, large and white and neatly trimmed. He glances next door. The Rickeys' house has a FOR SALE sign perched on the lawn, and all the lights are off. They had daughters that he went to school with, Mindy and Randi Rickey. He thinks of them and their slightly bucktoothed grins, pug noses, skinny legs. They are off at schools in New England too. He wonders, horrified, if he is suddenly related to them. At least he never dated either of them. Would that be retroactive incest? Maybe he did kiss Mindy once, at a party in someone's dark basement rec room. He did. It hits him with great clarity. She tasted like grape bubble gum and smelled like coconut hair spray. The combination nauseated him, but they definitely used their tongues.

His mother's voice sails across the front lawn. "Elliot? Is that you lurking out there?"

"I'm not lurking," Elliot mutters.

"Yes. You are," she calls. "You're lurking."

He doesn't know what to expect when he walks inside. After all, someone new has moved in—and not just anyone, but Mr. Rickey, whom Elliot has seen shirtless mowing his old lawn, his back covered with patches of reddish blond hair and freckles; whose daughter Elliot has French-kissed; whose wife used to overtip when Elliot was the neighborhood paperboy. And his mother is pregnant, almost out of her first trimester is how she put it, and he expects her to be glowing and round, Buddha-like.

But, to his surprise, everything is the same. The slate blue kitchen, the smell of Pine-Sol, the one chipped tile on the floor with its corner cut like someone stole a taste of pie. His mother has on faded jeans, an old pink button-down of his father's, bare feet. She is an L. L. Bean mother, just like the ones who fill that catalogue—long and straight hipped, blunt-cut hair that's close to blond, practical clothes, sensible face. Once, before his parents got divorced, Elliot heard his father accuse her of not being pretty enough. He was right; she was what you would call handsome, but never pretty. Still, it wasn't something men told the women they loved. Even at ten Elliot had known that.

"Well, hello," she says. She is planting bulbs—forcing them is what she calls it—and doesn't stop to welcome him.

Elliot kisses her cheek and notices she has acne, that she's covered it with a too-pink makeup.

"Good," she says. "I worried about Georgia getting you there on time."

He picks up an apple from the Bennington Potters bowl that sits on the counter, and takes a noisy bite. "She was early," he lies.

"Bravo," his mother says. "And here you are."

From somewhere in the cavernous house he hears Bach's Brandenburg Concertos.

"As soon as I finish forcing these bulbs," she tells him, "we'll get on with things."

"Things?" Elliot asks.

"You have to call your father, of course. Make plans to see him at some point. And I thought we'd all go for dinner at Duck's tonight."

Since their divorce, his parents haven't spoken except to discuss when Elliot would get dropped off and picked up and where. He can't imagine why they would all go to dinner. His father has lived on the Upper West Side with a woman, Veronica, since he left. Veronica looks exactly like the old movie star Louise Brooks. She does that on purpose, then acts surprised when people go up to her and say, "You look exactly like Louise Brooks!"

"We who?" Elliot manages to ask.

"Franklin and you and me," his mother says.

Franklin is Mr. Rickey. Elliot knows that from delivering his newspapers. H. Franklin Rickey. He realizes that he doesn't even know if his mother is Mrs. H. Franklin Rickey now, or if she kept her old name, Pamela Stern. He realizes that although everything looks the same and smells the same, it's all different. When Mr. Rickey appears in the kitchen, smiling dopily, his thin hair combed over his bald spot, his glasses smudged, his feet bare too, Elliot wants to run out of there.

"Elliot," he says. "Good to see you."

"Done!" his mother announces. She steps back to study her planting. "In six weeks this entire pot will be filled with paper whites. Lovely little things. Just in time for Christmas."

The three of them stand there and stare at the terra-cotta planter, which, although her prediction is accurate, looks like a bunch of onions stuck in a lot of dirt. They stare at it much longer than necessary.

ELLIOT IS MAJORING in English, but he can do math. Mr. Rickey got his mother pregnant first, and married her second. Over fish en papillote at Duck's, he thinks back to the summer, which was too hot and too long. Elliot worked odd jobs, as a tutor, a playground crafts director, and a picture developer at a one-hour photo place. In between, he lay on the green-striped sofa in the family room or on a chaise by the unfilled pool or in the hammock. He didn't read much. He saw his friends sometimes. He spent Fourth of July with his father and Veronica on their roof, where they had a barbecue because even though his father has lived in Manhattan for eight years, he can't let go of his suburban life—he keeps a car and shops at malls and has barbecues on rooftops. During all this, Elliot's mother was somehow, somewhere, fucking Mr. Rickey. "The Rickeys are having trouble," she told Elliot sadly. On Friday nights, she and Mr. Rickey had dinner here at Duck's. But she was always home and in her pajamas, her half-glasses perched on her nose, a book opened, when Elliot got home.

They are acting like they are in love, his mother and Mr. Rickey. They keep touching, intimately, knees and hands, and even gently bumping foreheads. Mr. Rickey is drinking too much, almost a whole bottle of wine himself.

"It's so different having a baby now," Elliot's mother tells him. She has taken small sips from Mr. Rickey's wineglass all night. "When I had you, I still had a martini whenever I wanted one. I got knocked out during delivery. I had never even seen my cervix."

They bump foreheads and giggle.

"These days, they make a point of including you in everything. We're going to Lamaze classes together. Fran will cut the umbilical cord. The works."

Embarrassed, Elliot looks down at his fish until his mother says, "You know who did all this way back when? Georgia. You know she had a child, don't you?"

He looks up and nods, suddenly interested.

His mother lowers her voice and leans across the table. "At the time I thought she was crazy, of course, but she had it with a midwife, and this woman made her squat like she was in a field or something, made her stay naked the whole time, and made her chant these Indian birthing songs while she rubbed her perineum with eucalyptus oil. Georgia says it wasn't so bad."

"Squatting?" Mr. Rickey asks. It is clear he cannot imagine such a thing.

Elliot's mother says, "Something about gravity."

"But she gave that baby away," Elliot reminds her.

"She never even held him."

"Tragic, really," Mr. Rickey says, shaking his head.

Elliot's mother has returned to her perfect posture. Her cheeks are slightly flushed, there is potting soil under her fingernails. She opens her small oval purse and pulls out a bad Polaroid that she slides across the table to Elliot. Mr. Rickey kneads her neck. They both grin.

The picture is dark, blurry. A picture of a night sky, perhaps. Or airplane radar.

"That's Tatiana or Alexander," she says proudly. "Of

course we'll find out the sex. Why not? They can tell you nowadays, you know."

It sinks in slowly: this is a photograph of their baby. Tatiana or Alexander? Why the Russian names? Elliot wonders. Then he remembers that Mr. Rickey has something to do with Russia. His old house was filled with those dolls that sit inside each other and ornate, painted Easter eggs. Once a year he and the real Mrs. Rickey used to have a party with caviar and borscht and thirty different kinds of vodka. Maybe he was even a spy.

Elliot's mother points to a place with her dirty fingernail and says, "That's the heart."

"Looks just like you," Elliot tells her, and slides the picture back across the table.

"He inherited his sarcasm from his father," she tells Mr. Rickey.

"Elliot," Mr. Rickey says, taking his mother's hand in both of his, "your mother and I would like you to join us at the birth of our child."

"It's allowed," Elliot's mother says. "We can make a whole list of people."

Elliot wonders if Mindy and Randi Rickey will be there too. It doesn't seem right.

"Don't worry," Mr. Rickey says, "no squatting and chanting."

Elliot can see it, Georgia squatting naked, her teeth gritted, pushing out her baby, chanting. But he can't understand what his mother and Mr. Rickey want from him, can't picture his mother naked and panting or doing any of it. The busboy picks up the dirty plates and smiles at Elliot, oddly, when he whisks his away.

"Georgia said they massaged her with honey," his mother whispers to Mr. Rickey.

Georgia's baby could be anyone, Elliot thinks. He could be here at Duck's eating dinner with his adopted parents. He could be the busboy. Anyone at all.

ON THANKSGIVING MORNING Elliot's mother and Mr. Rickey show up smelling like fish.

"I'm doing a bouillabaisse," his mother announces.

"Not a turkey?" Elliot says.

It is unseasonably warm, too warm for all the sweaters he packed, so he is wearing an old golf shirt of his father's, a kelly green clingy thing. He feels ridiculous.

"What are you wearing?" his mother says, holding a lobster in the air.

"All I want to know is why we're not having turkey," Elliot insists. "And cranberries and mashed potatoes." He doesn't mention the yams topped with marshmallows that she usually makes just for him.

"Well," she says slowly, like she's talking to a stupid person, "Mindy and Randi are having Thanksgiving with their mother in Katonah, and we thought that we'd make something else so they wouldn't have to force down two entire turkey dinners."

Those yams had brown sugar and molasses on them too. They had them every Thanksgiving Elliot can remember.

His mother has started to slam things on the counter— New Zealand mussels and jumbo shrimp and oysters still in their shells. "If you can't enjoy bouillabaisse with us, then maybe you should have Thanksgiving with your father."

"He's eating at a restaurant," he tells her.

"Well," she says, staring at him from under her bangs, "there you have it."

"Bouillabaisse," Elliot mutters, and stomps out, into the mudroom where an array of outdoorwear hangs on chunky hooks. No one ever got their own winter coat or ski jacket. Instead, his mother bought half a dozen in different colors and they grabbed whatever they needed. The same with rain boots and aqua socks and hiking shoes. They stood, orphans, in a neat row beneath the bench in the mudroom.

Today Elliot grabs a red down vest that is a little snug under the armpits and heads outside into the bright sun. Al Roker had promised balmy weather and he was right. Elliot cuts across the Rickeys' backyard, all overgrown and swampy from clogged gutters. Those Russian parties used to be held out here, he remembered. Mrs. Rickey used to serve the vodka in frozen blocks. Once, a few years ago, his mother had told him—cattily, Elliot decides now—that it wasn't such a big deal. "She fills an empty milk carton with water, sticks the bottle inside, and freezes the whole thing. Then she cuts away the milk carton and acts like she's done something monumental." Elliot pauses near the sliding glass doors that lead into the Rickeys' kitchen. Was his mother already fucking him back then?

The Rickeys' kitchen looks like someone still lives there. There is a vase of dried flowers on the table; a digital clock on the stove glows the correct time in red; and when Elliot presses his ear to the glass, he thinks he hears the clunky hum of the refrigerator, like an airplane about to take off. Theirs used to do that too. When they kicked it, it quieted, until eventually it broke down completely.

He wants nothing more than to go inside the Rickeys' house and poke around. Maybe he would find a pair of his mother's white cotton underpants under the bed, or a smudge of her pink lipstick somewhere private. Elliot jiggles the door until it opens, and steps inside. The first thing he does is kick the refrigerator and, after a gush of water drops from the ice-maker part, it shuts up. It smells a little rancid, like old fruit, and he sees that the dried flowers are actually just dead, not some Martha Stewart centerpiece idea. A card propped against the vase says, *Happy Anniversary, Babushka! Love, Fran.* He puts the card in the pocket of his jeans and wanders through other rooms.

Unlike Elliot's house, the Rickeys' sprawls like a wide yawn, all on one floor with little steps here and there. Elliot has to step down into the living room, up into the dining room. It's a house where people would fall a lot, he decides, stumbling. The den has, standing almost as tall as Elliot, one of those Russian dolls with the other dolls inside. When he gets closer, he recognizes that it's Gorbachev. It takes two hands to untwist and remove Gorbachev's head, and when he finally does, the next doll is Bush. To the Rickeys, this was probably very funny. Elliot wanders out of the den, past two closed doors, and into the master bedroom, still holding Gorbachev's head.

The bed is stripped, the bureau tops are dusty, and the drawers and closets gape open, empty except for crumpled tissues, pennies, and twisted coat hangers. He sets Gorbachev's head on the tall chest of drawers and stretches out on the bed. He's surprised when he picks up the phone and gets a dial tone. The only number he can think to call is his old buddy Rhett, who has dropped out or flunked out of six colleges in two years.

Rhett is happy to hear from him. "Are you back?" he asks.

"Remember Mindy and Randi Rickey?" Elliot whispers. "I'm at their house. Next door to mine."

"I thought that family moved or something," Rhett says.

"The house is abandoned except for some former world leaders."

"Like, empty?" Rhett says.

"Yeah." Elliot looks around. "Empty."

"Cool. I've got some killer weed. I'll bring it over and we can get really wasted before dinner." This is why Rhett can't finish a semester in one place.

"Cool," Elliot says.

While he waits for Rhett to show up, Elliot wanders back through the house, opening the two closed doors as he goes. They were probably Mindy's and Randi's rooms, but now they too are empty—stripped beds, gaping closets. The refrigerator is acting up again, so he goes back to the kitchen and gives it a kick. Those dead flowers are bugging him. Elliot takes them out of the vase and throws them in the trash compactor. How could Mr. Rickey give his wife an anniversary bouquet while he was fucking Elliot's mother? Elliot imagines Mrs. Rickey, with her pale blond hair and round reddish cheeks, arranging the flowers in her good crystal vase. He imagines her smiling, humming even, thinking she's still his babushka, that he still loves her.

The refrigerator won't shut up this time, no matter how hard Elliot kicks. When he opens the door to give it a good hard slam, he sees the freezer is lined in neat rows with milk cartons that have bottles of vodka stuck in them, frozen into blocks. There are maybe a dozen in there. It takes three trips to the master bedroom to carry them all. Unlike Mrs. Rickey, Elliot doesn't cut off the milk cartons. He just screws off the caps and pours all the vodka into Gorbachev's head.

By the time Rhett shows up, Elliot has consumed quite a bit. It's icy and smooth and tastes like water.

"Whoa," Rhett says when he sees Elliot drinking from Gorbachev's head. "That is totally fucking weird."

"I don't know," Elliot says. "I think they were spies or something. This is all Russian vodka." His hands sweep dramatically, the way they do when he's well on his way to being good and drunk, pointing out all the empty bottles sticking out of those milk cartons.

"Who is that anyway?" Rhett asks, pointing to the head with the joint he's brought. "Stalin or somebody?"

"No, no," Elliot tells him. "See the birthmark."

Rhett looks at it upside down, twisting his own head. "Whoa," he says again, and lights up.

The joint and the vodka loosen Elliot's tongue. He wants to say things out loud, but instead he closes his eyes and imagines Georgia naked. Once, briefly, Elliot saw his own mother naked. He opened the bathroom door and there she was, standing in front of the mirror, her arms stretched up over her head, staring at herself. Her flesh was pink from a hot shower, her stomach bulged slightly, like a pouch. She turned toward him as if she were expecting someone. Elliot closed the door, fast, and ran down the hall to his own room, nauseated. But Georgia naked in his mind takes on the body of the girls his age, the ones he's seen. And he knows, watching her there, swimming in his spinning brain, that if he touched Georgia, she would be smooth like them, taut.

"What are you doing? Jerking off?" Rhett says, nudging Elliot with his foot. "You're moaning, man."

Elliot opens his eyes and watches the ceiling spin. He is one of the few people he knows who like having the spins.

Rhett's eyes are bloodshot, the lids drooping. "Fucking Thanksgiving," he mutters.

THEY STUMBLE BACK across the Rickeys' old yard, toward home. But instead of going in, they go to the dining room window and watch. Mindy and Randi Rickey are seated side by side, dressed in black mini-dresses, looking funereal. Elliot can actually see the steam rising from the bouillabaisse. He's hungry, but unable to propel himself inside.

"They look like a family," Elliot says.

"This is when I'm glad I'm adopted," Rhett whispers. "I feel no familial obligation."

Elliot's already dry throat turns drier. "Adopted?" he croaks.

Rhett shrugs and keeps watching. Elliot sees that his usual chair is empty and sad.

"Do you know who your mother is?" Elliot asks, noticing the reflection of his frown over the tureen. Georgia made that tureen for his mother one Christmas. It is lumpy, ugly, misshapen, and his mother hates it.

"Who cares?" Rhett answers. He is watching Elliot's mother, too.

Between them sits Gorbachev's head, vodka sloshing around inside it.

"All I know is the adoption was in New York. Private," Rhett says.

In that moment Elliot is certain that Rhett's mother is Georgia. He has the same springy black hair, the same "fuck it" attitude. He keeps watching his own mother, raising a glass in a toast. Is she even missing me? Elliot wonders. He feels invisible, erased. There are the Rickeys in his dining room, a new Rickey in his mother's stomach, and him nowhere, unmissed.

"What if I told you I might know who your real mother is?" Elliot whispers.

He waits for an answer, but Rhett has slipped away, into the darkness. He is alone.

LIKE A BURGLAR, Elliot eases back inside. Still stoned and drunk, he has to hold the wall with one hand for support as he makes his way through the house. Nothing has changed, not really. There are men's shoes in the den, the smell of foot powder creeping out of them. On the coffee table, an almost empty snifter of brandy, a pipe, a *Sail* magazine. Elliot finishes off the brandy and with it gets a taste of cherry pipe-tobacco. He goes from familiar room to familiar room, but sees nothing else out of place.

Upstairs, he hesitates at the guest room door. For years, before he moved out, that was where his father slept. But now, it is the lumps of the Rickey sisters that he sees when he peers inside, frowning against the darkness.

"Hey," Elliot says in his normal tone of voice.

One of the lumps moves, shifts, but the voice comes from the other one.

"Elliot?" she says.

"How was the bouillabaisse?" he asks.

"I'm allergic," she says. "To all fish and seafood. If I eat it, I swell and ultimately choke." She sighs, and Elliot hears her settle back into the pillows and blankets. He does not know which sister she is, but he doesn't want her to go to sleep.

"I have some great vodka," he says. "In the backyard."

"Is that where you've been?" she says. Elliot remembers the expressionless tone of this particular Rickey sister; he just doesn't remember which one possesses it. "Drinking vodka?" she continues, her voice flat.

"Come on," he says, whispering suddenly.

Even in the dim hall light, seeing her face to face, Elliot does not know which sister this is. Her face has red sleeplines on one side, her hair on that side is slightly matted.

"This Thanksgiving has been awful," she says as they wander through the quiet house and into the backyard, where Gorbachev's head leans drunkenly against the back steps.

"Hey," she says, "we used to have one of those too."

Elliot tips it forward so she can drink, then drinks more himself. The buzz he had has turned into a dull headache.

"My mother is a mess," she says with her flat voice. She stretches out on the grass. The air has turned cooler, damp, and her nipples are hard against the white cotton nightgown she wears.

Elliot thinks of books like *Wuthering Heights*; this

Rickey sister on the grass could be a heroine from a novel like that, her hair fanning out around her, all that white. He drinks more, then thrusts his hand beneath her nightgown. She doesn't have on any underwear, and her pubic hair surprises him. Elliot pulls his hand back.

"Yes," she says, sitting up and pulling her nightgown over her head. "Let's do that. Maybe it will help this rotten day."

But, of course, it doesn't. While Elliot is on her, his knees digging into the grass and dirt, he thinks he hears sounds from the house. He thinks there is light coming from upstairs, illuminating them, there on the grass, capturing this dispassionate act. And when they are done—finally, Elliot catches himself thinking—when he can finally turn around, he sees that there is a light on, his mother's bedroom light.

He looks at the Rickey sister beside him, naked on the lawn, crying silently.

"I hate you, you know," she says. "I hate your whole rotten family."

Rotten, he thinks. And he thinks of his father and Veronica, of his mother upstairs with Mr. Rickey, of what he himself has just done.

"We were happy, you know," she continues, crying harder now. Elliot remembers the bouquet on their kitchen table, the note. "Your mother's a whore. A rotten whore."

This shocks him. The girl is passionate now, sitting up, trembling.

"Do you know how long she'd been sleeping with my father? Three years. And when he didn't leave my mother, she went and got herself pregnant so he would."

Foolishly, Elliot covers himself with his shirt. "What?" he manages.

"My parents fought about her for three years. The way he used to sneak over here to fuck her in the middle of the night—"

"Hey," Elliot says. "That's not right." But somewhere inside him he knows that it is right. All the numbers add up only this way. His mother stretching, naked, waiting for someone. The comments after those Russian parties. The suddenness of all this change. The baby.

"Oh, it's right, Elliot. It's right," she says, struggling to her feet and making her way back to the house, naked.

He does not move. In the light from his mother's bedroom window, Elliot watches her go, wonders who she is.

VERONICA AND HIS father are arguing about worms and how they reproduce. His father has bought an entire series of educational videos on animal sex. Elliot remembers the Rickey girl beneath him last night and feels nauseated.

"Worms," Veronica is saying, "are both. Male and female. They fuck themselves." Veronica loves to say "fuck." She uses it whenever she can.

His father throws his hands up, exasperated. "They're better off than we are, then, aren't they, Elliot?"

They are eating lunch at an overpriced restaurant in the Village. His father is acting like a country bumpkin, mispronouncing items on the menu, ordering beer and drinking it straight from the bottle. And now this, fighting with Veronica, loudly, about the sex habits of worms. Elliot is hungover and has small splinters in his lips from drinking out of Gorbachev's head, but somehow he feels enlightened.

Perhaps, he thinks, startled, his father is uncouth, perhaps he always has been, with his sherbet-colored clothes and loud, overly enthusiastic voice.

"This salad," his father is saying, "is going to send me straight into cardiac arrest." He picks at it. "Too much bacon."

"Lardons," Veronica says. She lights up a cigarette and inhales deeply, even though they are all still eating.

"Whatever," his father says, and waves his fork around, sending lardons and some lettuce—"Free-zays," his father had called it when he'd ordered—flying onto the floor. Ignoring it, he leans toward Elliot. "Cholesterol, hypertension, blah blah blah. You can't relax for a minute."

Veronica is gazing at everyone else in the restaurant, her eyes flickering, settling, moving on.

"Now there's all this safe sex you have to worry about," Elliot's father continues in his boisterous, "atta boy" voice.

Elliot looks around too, embarrassed. He remembers a night out with his parents back before they got divorced. They went to a new Japanese restaurant for sushi and his father kept squinting his eyes and saying, "Ah so," as if it were the biggest joke in the world. His mother had gotten up, gathered her jacket and purse, and left, her head bent, her cheeks red. But Elliot and his father had sat and finished their dinner, had taken their time, really. Elliot had been surprised to find his mother sitting in the car when they went out to the parking lot. Somehow he had expected her to be home, gone. But she was sitting in the front seat, looking out the window, waiting.

"Do you?" his father is asking, and Elliot realizes he missed some important part of a conversation.

"What?" he says.

"Do you have safe sex? Use condoms? Whatever?"

Elliot looks around again, certain that everyone is listening.

"Of course," he lies, thinking again of the Rickey sister last night. This morning he had been unable to get the grass stains off his knees.

Veronica leans back in her chair, blows a long stream of smoke, and says, "Cats have barbed penises, you know."

At least she spoke softly, Elliot thinks, grateful.

"That's why they scream that way during sex. It hurts," Veronica says, studying him.

His father laughs. "You've got to see these videos, Elliot."

ELLIOT WALKS UP and down Bank Street, trying to find Georgia's old building. He is certain of the block, but all the brownstones look the same. Sitting on a stoop, he wishes he could find Georgia herself, wishes he could lose himself in her black curls, her sex smell. He imagines what her breasts would look like, feel like, taste like, imagines himself suckling on them, drawing out the long, hard nipple, feeding off her. Like a baby, he finds himself thinking.

All these years, Elliot's fantasies about Georgia have been sexual. In junior high, his wet dreams alternated between Kristie Madden, a science whiz with strawberry blond hair and freckles, and Georgia. Suddenly, he is imagining something else, something more. He thinks of his father and how embarrassed he had made him feel; he thinks of his mother stealing Mr. Rickey away from his family. Is that who he's a part of? Or is he someone else, cut loose from them, really, taken in?

Elliot closes his eyes and pictures himself inside Georgia. In the past, he has imagined himself there often, riding her, thrusting himself into her. But this is different; he thinks of floating in her, the way this new baby floats inside his mother, cushioned there, warm, safe. He imagines sliding out of her, Georgia squatting and pushing until he emerges. For an instant, it does not feel like pretending. It feels real. Maybe, Elliot thinks, maybe it is real, a buried memory. Maybe these two other people had nothing to do with him at all. Thinking it, he feels light, uplifted, hopeful.

He stands, knowing what he has to do.

AT THE END of the day, St. Gregory's Hospital is empty, the air thick with pine-scented floor cleaner and old urine. For almost seventy-five years, St. Gregory's has served as an orphanage, a place where unwed mothers could have their babies and give them away, or bring their children and leave them for someone else to take home. It was where Georgia had sent her son; Elliot knows that because every time they passed St. Gregory's his mother told him about Georgia's child, how she never even held him, how a transfer here had been made, and someone had, presumably, adopted him.

Waiting for someone to appear at the records office to help him, Elliot hopes for another rush of memory, a sign that he has been here once, briefly, before he was transferred over to the people who had raised him. Already, in the short subway ride uptown, the faces of his parents have dimmed, his connection to them has grown frayed and thin.

There is nothing modern about St. Gregory's. Thick, dusty files line the room that stretches before him beyond the desk where he waits. The telephones have rotary dials. *I'm like a time traveler,* Elliot thinks, smiling. He hears someone approaching, slowly, shuffling along the newly washed floors. He hears his mother's constant reprimand when he was a child: *Pick up your feet, Elliot. Don't drag them like that.* He thinks too of Georgia and the clogs she always used to wear. She clopped when she walked, heavy, noisy. His mother used to wonder aloud at home how someone could wear those things, why someone would wear them. "They aren't even attractive," she'd say, shaking her head, looking down at her own practical loafers. Elliot used to like it best when Georgia wore no shoes at all and padded around her Bank Street apartment barefoot, the pads of her feet thick and callused, her arches so high that she always appeared to be about to jump.

A voice behind him says, "I can guess why you're here."

Elliot turns to face a small, wizened nun, dressed in a black habit, bent almost in two, her back like a bridge in a Japanese garden.

"They all come back," she says, shuffling past him, to the desk.

"They who?" Elliot says.

Once, in an adult education class at the local high school, his mother took a course in making figures out of dried apples. She made a woman, dressed it in a long red-print dress and white bonnet, put a doll-size butter churn in its hand. That apple woman's face looked just like this nun's: wrinkled and dried so much that it appears to be folded like that, pressed into its own peculiar shape.

"The children," the nun says, shaking her head. "The little ones who were given away."

Elliot fights back an urge to touch her, to stroke that dried-apple face. He longs for arms around him, he realizes. He longs to be held. He thinks he might cry, so he merely nods.

"I have cancer," the nun says without self-pity. "Of the stomach. They say my intestines have disintegrated, that they're just hanging there, loose, like old yarn. I can only tolerate applesauce and baby food." She shakes her head, as if remembering. "Not even water will stay down," she continues. "Do you know what I used to love? Pizza! With pepperoni!" Her eyes sparkle. "I always used to add extra hot pepper flakes." She starts to shuffle away from him, to the room beyond. She pauses. "Name?"

"Elliot Stern," he says.

"No, no, no. Do you know your mother's name, sonny?"

"Georgia," Elliot says, his voice barely above a whisper. "Montenegro."

The nun nods, then disappears between those shelves, her feet leaving smeared footprints in the dust.

While he waits for her to return, Elliot considers all the possibilities that lay before him. He will never have to go back to the house in Chappaqua, where, when he left this morning, his mother and Mr. Rickey had started to paint his father's old study a color called celery, which his mother had read soothed infants. He will never have to endure another meal with his father and Veronica, with their arguing and Veronica's smoking while he eats and his father's slapping him on the back. He will never have to face the Rickey sisters in daylight. He could go back to

Providence tonight, ring Georgia's doorbell, lose himself
in her arms, in her hug. Thinking it, he can almost actually
feel those arms around him. She never got to hold him, he
remembers.

The nun comes back with a file, thin, dusty, sealed.

In front of him she breaks the seal and opens the folder.

"Baby boy Montenegro," she reads. "April 16, 1975.
Mother: Georgia A. Father: Unknown. Adopted April 23,
1975, by Margaret M. and Alexander D. Lewis, 10 Bank
Street, New York, New York."

The information rattles around in his brain. None of it is
him. Not the birthday—his is in January—or the names of
the adopted parents. He is not Georgia's son, after all. The
feeling of her embrace vanishes and he is left shivering, as the
nun hands him the file and shuffles out.

"Send me more," she says. "I'll tell them. I don't want
these babies walking around the earth alone, untethered."

But he is, Elliot realizes. He is alone and untethered.

ELLIOT DRAGS GORBACHEV'S head from the backyard,
where he left it, up to his room. The temperature has
dropped and a thin layer of ice has formed across the top of
the vodka that was left. Like an ice fisherman, Elliot breaks
through it, then begins to drink, lying naked on his bed in his
room. He wonders if Georgia had known she was living a
few blocks from her son all those years. Had she moved
there to watch him grow up after all? He does not remember
any children his age on those long-ago Saturday trips to
Manhattan and Georgia's apartment. But why would he?

They had only sat up there, listening to Georgia talk, trying to sort out the loose ends of her life.

When the bedroom door opens, the smell of fresh paint floats in.

"It's me," the Rickey sister says.

It is the same one as last night. She has on the same long, white nightgown, but as soon as she closes the door she takes it off and, naked, climbs onto the bed with him. He hands her Gorbachev's head, and she gulps from it.

When she hands it back, she wipes her mouth with the back of her hand and says, "We used to have one like this."

"You told me that already," Elliot says.

"Where's the rest? There's a bottom and other dolls, you know."

"I know. They're next door."

"At my house?" she says in her flat voice.

Elliot nods.

"You mean this is ours?" she says.

He nods again.

"Is that what your entire family does? They take things that aren't theirs? What kind of people are you?"

"I don't know," he says.

She drinks more, taking in huge gulps. "The point here is to get totally wasted," she says.

After he left St. Gregory's, Elliot went to a phone booth and called information, looking for an Alexander Lewis in Manhattan on Bank Street, then just in Manhattan, then in Queens, Brooklyn, the Bronx, Staten Island. He was desperate to find Georgia's son. He checked for a Margaret Lewis. He checked for them in Long Island and Westchester and Albany and New Jersey and Connecticut. He began to call random Informations—Denver, Seattle, Miami. But the Lewises had disappeared.

"It's working," the Rickey sister is saying. "I'm getting drunk this fast. This is good to know. That it's possible to do this."

He takes the head from her and drinks.

"My mother is so depressed," she says. "She's on Prozac. Can you believe that? She told us everything. How once she came home and found your mother fucking my father in their bed. In my parents' bed, I mean. During the day. And another time, during one of their Russian Night parties, she went downstairs to get more ice, and they were doing it right on the floor. Like animals, my mother said." Her words are starting to slur. "She said she took him back time and again because she loved him, but it was like your mother had put a spell on him. He'd apologize and promise never to do it again, but then she'd start calling, asking him to come over, to do this or that."

Elliot tries to imagine this vixen mother she is describing. His mother wears white cotton underwear, for God's sake. She wears chinos. How sexy is that?

The Rickey sister is looming over him now, her face pasty and drunk looking, sloppy. "He told my mother, 'She's in my blood. I'm sorry.' Then my parents went to Russia to make amends. My mother is a forgiving person—"

"A saint," Elliot says.

"Yes. That's right. A saint. They went to Russia and came back in love and your mother went nuts. She took a key and scratched my mother's car. Her Saab. Ran a key along one whole side."

"My mother?" Elliot says.

"She freaked out. She called him all night sometimes.

She threatened to kill herself if he didn't come over. And he resisted."

Elliot tries to imagine this. All the while he was at Brown, was this going on? As he wandered along Thayer Street at night, half stoned, peering into the weird fluorescent lights of the Gap, was his mother doing these things? Or even last summer, while he worked his ridiculous jobs and wasted time?

"And then one night my mother wakes up. It's hot. Summer. And my father isn't in bed. She thinks maybe he's sick. The heat gets to him, you know? So she starts looking for him. She looks around the whole house, and he's not there and she's worried. Then from somewhere outside she hears this sound, this kind of screaming, and she thinks it's two cats fucking on the lawn but then she hears my father's name, and she steps outside and follows the sounds right to your yard. They're coming from your whore mother's bedroom and that's where my father is and that's when she got knocked up. Okay? Are you happy?"

"No," Elliot says.

He puts his arms around her and holds her the way he wants to be held. He rocks her, soothes her. And later, when she throws up, he holds her head and strokes her hair and cleans up after her and lets her kiss him sloppily on the mouth. He tastes her vomit, her cold tongue fills him, and even though she's drunk and smells of puke, he pulls her on top of him and makes love like it's his only desire, like it matters. When he comes, he opens his mouth and lets his cry fill the air.

"GEORGIA," ELLIOT WHISPERS into the phone, to the blankness of an answering machine at the other end. "Georgia. Pick up, please. It's me. It's Elliot."

As long as he keeps talking, the machine will listen; it isn't one of those that cut you off after thirty seconds. He stands, naked, in the hallway, the phone cord stretched taut. The air smells of stale vomit and the fish from yesterday's bouillabaisse.

"Everything here is so weird," he whispers, realizing he has nothing to say, really. Outside the window at the end of the hallway, Elliot sees snow starting to fall, small, dizzy flakes bombarding the glass. "It's snowing all of a sudden," he says.

The hall light comes on, blinding him, and in it stands his mother.

"I love you," he whispers into the phone. He doesn't want to hang up, to end the connection, so he just stands there, clutching it to his chest the way, as a child, he'd clutched his worn and faded baby blanket.

"Elliot," his mother says, averting her eyes.

She is wearing a long, red plaid nightshirt that makes her look, suddenly, ridiculously, young. And pregnant, Elliot realizes. Her breasts, her belly, are swollen and round. He feels embarrassed for all of them.

"Is Mindy Rickey in there?" his mother is asking him. She still looks away from him, even as she points to his room behind him.

"I don't know," he answers honestly. Then says, "Yes. I guess so." He slumps down to the floor, dropping the phone, letting his back trace the wall as he slides. He imagines that the blue flowers on the wallpaper are real, imagines their thorns slicing into him.

Now that his nakedness is partially hidden, his mother advances, glaring, her nostrils flared. Elliot remembers how, when he used to get mad at her, he would mutter, "Pig nose," and it made him feel better.

"What is it you're trying to prove exactly?" his mother hisses. She stands over him like a balloon in the Macy's parade, inflated, too large.

"Me?" he asks. "What am *I* trying to prove?"

"Do you think I'm deaf?" she says, her voice rising. "Do you think I'm blind?"

Out of the blue, he remembers something. He remembers Mrs. Rickey's black Saab 900 sitting in her driveway last summer with a key scratch down its side. He remembers his mother shaking her head as they passed it, and saying, "What a shame. Such a nice car too."

"Last night right outside my window. And tonight in my own house. Have you no respect at all?"

"You did it," Elliot says, stunned, even a little awed.

"I did it?"

"You scratched Mrs. Rickey's car last summer." Saying it, he realizes that it all must be true. He studies his mother's face, trying to recognize something in it.

Her mouth opens, then shuts again, several times, like a fish gasping for air.

The house has changed, turned cold. Elliot feels himself coiling, folding, trying to find warmth somehow. But he can't. His mother moves, slightly awkwardly, down to the floor beside him.

"You don't know the first thing about it," she says, weary. "Someday you'll fall in love and maybe then you'll understand."

"What a useless, ridiculous thing to say," Elliot says.

They sit like this a moment more, neither of them talking. Then his mother gets up, awkward again. He watches her carefully, her pig nose, her straight bangs and blunt hair. Her lips are chapped. Her nails are square. These things are all familiar, yet he does not know her.

From the dangling telephone, a voice is screaming. "Elliot? Elliot? What the hell is going on?"

Elliot picks it up and places it, gently, back into the cradle.

THE SNOW IS accumulating quickly. He has carried Gorbachev's head out with him. Finally, it is empty; all the vodka has been drunk. Elliot wants to return it to the Rickeys' house, where it belongs. With so much snow, the walk is slippery. There is little moonlight. He is on his own.

When Elliot looks behind him, his footprints are already covered. It is as if he is the first one to walk here, ever. He imagines it. Pausing, he looks back at his own house, dark again. What would the first person to see it think? Would he think there was love inside? Would he believe how much had been risked there? Gorbachev's head feels light in his arms. Like a blanket, like an infant. He raises it above his own head and slips it on, letting it settle over his head, resting on his shoulders. Like a cocoon, Elliot thinks. It is so silent inside that he can hear his own breath, his own heartbeat, even the blood pulsing in his veins. He stands there and listens. He listens hard.

NEW PEOPLE

MARJORIE MACOMBER IS stretched out on a chaise lounge
in her backyard, eyeing the new boy her husband hired to
take care of the lawn. She is wet with Hawaiian Tropic suntan oil; she is pretending to read a home decorating magazine; she is thinking the boy is too young, too sexy, too
trashy to be here, in her yard, distracting her. His name is
Justin, one of those soap opera names people give their children. He is shirtless, tanned, tattooed. He makes Marjorie
nervous.

The Macombers live in a big white house with stone pil-
lars in the front that was built back in the forties. Some of the
neighbors—like the O'Haras next door—have divided up
their large lots and sold them off so that now new slapped-
together houses are wedged in between the older, better
homes. Marjorie has a burning distaste for these new people
and their boxy houses. They have come in and ruined the
neighborhood, which used to be quiet and friendly, the kind
of place where neighbors got together for barbecues in summer or skating parties in winter—and even the pond has
been filled in and sold; there's no place to skate now. Cissy

O'Hara used to babysit Marjorie's daughter Bonnie. Bonnie used to babysit the Hummers' three children down the street. That's the kind of place it was. Now people move in and out, build sloppy homes, fill their yards with junk.

The yard boy is one of these new people, Marjorie knows. Her husband mentioned he lived down the street, in the Exeters' yard, which means in a tacky little house in the part of the lot the Exeters sold off. Marjorie tries to focus on her magazine, but the boy is shearing the hedges nearby and he's noisy about it. She watches his muscles ripple, his shoulder blades roll, and wonders what in the world Gary had been thinking when he hired someone like this. Their last gardener was a kindly old Cambodian man named Phong, who moved in and out of their yard with great quiet and grace.

The boy is, suddenly, right in front of her.

"Hey," he says, "you know what time it is?"

Marjorie slowly lifts her sunglasses off her nose and slides them onto the top of her head.

"Almost noon," she says, pointing to the sky.

He follows her finger with his whole body, then turns back, smiling a smart-alecky grin. "Someone up there telling you something?"

She levels a stare at him, the one that used to send Bonnie running to her room but that has no effect on this kind of boy.

"The sun is directly overhead at noon," she tells him. She hears the condescension drip from her mouth and it makes her feel satisfied. He is a stupid, beautiful boy and she doesn't want him in her yard.

Justin looks back at the sun and then at her. "Cool," he says.

The shears droop like a gun from his left hand. His tattoos are sprawling and colorful—the yin and yang, a dead rock star, even a heart with a banner of roses and the name *Janis* written inside.

"Joplin," the boy says, startling Marjorie. He has caught her staring at his big arms and he grins a different, slyer grin now. This boy is used to girls wanting him; he's too cocky, too sure of himself.

"How interesting," Marjorie says, and lowers her sunglasses, hoping he doesn't see her hand tremble. From the safety of her Wayfarers, Marjorie takes in his face: angular, a good straight nose, full lips, and bright blue eyes. The eyes are surprising; his hair is very dark, as long as Bonnie's, and wavy.

"So," Justin says. "Is there anything else I can do for you?"

She can smell him, all sweat and earth and male.

"No," Marjorie manages.

From next door, there is the sound of children, splashing and squealing with delight. The people who live in the O'Haras' yard have two or three little girls, all with tangled hair and sunburns. The children always seem to have on clothing from a Disney movie—a Pocohantas tee shirt, *101 Dalmations* bathing suit, even the pool is decorated with *Lion King* characters. Marjorie wonders how the O'Haras can stand having them in their yard.

Justin is still standing there, close enough that Marjorie can see the dark curly hair on his legs.

She turns the page of her magazine.

"Are we paying you to stand around?" she says.

He grins again. What a wiseguy! Marjorie thinks, and decides she will insist that Gary fire him. Surely Phong has relatives, dozens of them, who could work here.

"You tell me," Justin says. His voice has a flat affectless quality that disturbs her. "I'll do whatever you want. Boss."

"Honestly," Marjorie says.

She gathers her things—magazines, bottled water, suntan oil—gets up, and walks away, aware of his eyes following her across the long expanse of green yard. There are neat lines where he's mowed. She hopes her bathing suit bottom isn't riding up on her, hopes that her thighs aren't jiggling at all, hopes that he understands exactly what kind of person she is.

MARJORIE AND GARY are eating on the patio. This summer, she has decided to serve only salads for dinner, and to eat out here whenever they can. She has citronella candles burning, the too bright outside light off. The salads tonight are mozzarella with fresh tomato and basil, and mixed greens with red onion and cannellini beans. There is sourdough bread, extra virgin olive oil, the pepper mill, all spread out on the table between Marjorie and Gary. Already Marjorie has had too much wine. She isn't drunk, but she is light-headed in a pleasant way.

"That boy," she says. "I don't like him."

One of the reasons she has kept the light out here off is so Gary won't sit and read the newspaper while they eat.

"Which boy?" Gary says. His white golf shirt seems to glow in the candlelight.

"Jason, Justin, whoever he is," Marjorie says, knowing it's Justin but wanting to demean him, even here with Gary. "He gives me the creeps."

"He's only charging five dollars an hour," Gary says.

"I liked Phong," Marjorie says. She is pouting a little; all that wine.

"Phong has some awful cancer," Gary says. "Bone cancer, I think. He certainly can't come and cut our grass with something like that."

She knows why they've lost Phong. She sent a fruit basket to his house.

From the yard next door, those children scream and play.

"Don't they ever go to bed?" Gary says, his voice hushed. "They're so . . ." He struggles for the word. "Untended," he says finally.

Gary's hair is silver, cut short. He is tall and lean, like he always has been, and he plays tennis and golf. Five years ago he quit smoking. He is aging well, Marjorie thinks, pleased.

It's just for the summer," Gary is saying.

"He's the sort of boy who will break into the house and kill us while we sleep," Marjorie says. She doesn't really believe this. But how can she tell Gary her real problem with the boy? "Like those Menendez brothers," she adds.

Gary laughs at her, affectionately. Even though she went to Wellesley and got a degree in English, he has always seen her as a scatterbrain. It charms him, this image of her.

"They killed their own parents," he says, reaching across all the food for her hand. "Not someone else's."

He follows her hand like it's a lifeline out of deep water, follows it around the table, holding on tight, until he is at her side. Then he lets go, and moves his hands onto her shoulders so that he can turn her toward him, then moves them inside her button down shirt and inside her bra until he finds each nipple. He is kissing her too, urging her off her chair down onto the stone patio.

"There are berries," Marjorie says. "For dessert."

Gary laughs. He is tugging on the zipper of his shorts.

"Here?" Marjorie whispers. "Not here." But she is taking off her own shirt and shorts and underwear.

From next door, a woman's voice, high, too shrill: *"Jessica! Jessica!"*

Gary has found his way inside her. Marjorie sees his tanned back, his white buttocks, clear in the candlelight.

"Jessica!"

The stone patio is hard and cold on Marjorie's back. Above her the stars seem to drip from the sky, toward her. She hears herself sigh. She closes her eyes. The silly tufts of gray hair that have sprouted on his shoulders and back in his middle age tickle her hands when she moves them there.

"Oooh," Gary whispers into her ear, his breath sharp with red onion. "I'm glad the little girls are having fun too."

Of course they aren't; one of them seems to be lost. But Marjorie doesn't care. She lifts her hips up to meet her husband.

ON WEDNESDAY MORNING Bonnie stops in for coffee. Like her mother, Bonnie is small boned, wiry. Her hair is the same dark blond Marjorie's once was; now Marjorie gets hers frosted so that it is more of a silvery blond. They both wear it in a blunt cut, collarbone length, with headbands or pulled back in ponytails, which is what they both have today. People used to think they were sisters.

Bonnie is a lawyer and lives on the East Side in Providence, in a condo in what used to be a church. She and her husband—a lawyer too—sank all their money into a beach house, where they disappear every weekend. All of these things make Marjorie proud of her daughter.

This morning Bonnie has brought Portuguese sweet rolls to have with their coffee.

"Daddy and I are just having salads for dinner these days," Marjorie tells her daughter. "This way I don't need to turn on anything—oven, stove, nothing. It's really made life simpler."

Bonnie smiles in a way that makes Marjorie think she has a secret.

"What?" Marjorie says. "I know you've got something up your sleeve."

Bonnie grabs both of her mother's hands. "I told Ted I'd wait because he thinks it's bad luck to tell too soon. But I can't keep it from you."

Marjorie gets a sick feeling in her bones. She knows, of course, what Bonnie is about to tell her and she knows it should make her delighted—*a grandchild!*—but she feels awful, like Bonnie is about to tell her *bad* news.

"You've guessed, haven't you?" Bonnie says, slightly deflated. "It's just six weeks. Hardly pregnant at all."

"There's no such thing as hardly pregnant," Marjorie says. "At any rate, Ted is right. Things can go wrong early on."

Bonnie looks horrified.

Marjorie pats her daughter's hand. "I'm sure you'll be fine," she tells her. Then takes their coffee cups to the sink. She wants Bonnie to leave. She says, "Rhoda Harris and I are going to play tennis today. Then have lunch." It's all a lie. She has no plans today. Rhoda Harris is in England with her husband.

Bonnie has come up behind her. "If I didn't know better," she says, "I'd think you weren't happy about my news."

"Don't be silly," Marjorie says, letting the water run too hot and plunging her hands under it. "It's just that if we get all excited and something goes wrong, we'll feel just terrible." Saying this, Marjorie realizes it is exactly what she wants, for something to go wrong, for there to be no baby. "It's wonderful news," she says, forcing herself to turn around and hug Bonnie. "Imagine! A new little person running around."

Happy now, Bonnie says, "I guess I should get to the office. I wish I'd get some morning sickness or something. I mean, I feel really wonderful."

Marjorie has always heard that's a bad sign, to have no symptoms. "You're sure?" she says.

Bonnie nods. "Positive."

Marjorie turns back to the dishes in the sink.

"Mother," Bonnie says, standing on tiptoe and peering over Marjorie's shoulder to see out the window. "Who is that young man?"

Marjorie glances up. "That is your father's idea of a gardener."

"What's happened to Phong?" Bonnie asks.

"He went and got sick and this is who Daddy replaces him with."

They both watch Justin push the lawn mower. He has on cutoff jeans and nothing else.

"He's like a Greek god," Bonnie says.

Marjorie laughs. "Hardly. He's practically illiterate and he has these terrible tattoos everywhere."

"I think he's very handsome," Bonnie says. "Maybe he can come and cut *our* grass at the beach."

"You would be very disappointed," Marjorie tells her.

Still, long after Bonnie leaves, she stands at the sink looking out, watching the way his muscles push against his skin. He hesitates at the white fence that separates their yard from the O'Haras'. Marjorie cranes her neck to see what it is he's doing there. For a moment she thinks he's pissing—his hands seem to flutter somewhere in front of him, his back arches oddly. There is a flower bed there, but he isn't stooping. The boy is pissing on her flowers, on the neat rows of anemones and petunias that she herself planted and that Phong tended for several summers. Marjorie isn't certain what she should do. But then the boy, with an elaborate shudder, moves away, lugging a large garbage bag. Still, Marjorie stands there until the doorbell rings, and leaves to answer it, disappointed.

Marjorie doesn't recognize the woman standing on her doorstep. But she recognizes the little girl clinging to her leg. These are the people next door, from the O'Haras' yard. The woman is pregnant—God! Marjorie thinks. Is everyone pregnant these days?—all white doughy flesh and bumpy cellulite thighs. She shouldn't be wearing shorts. Her toenails are bright pink. And the little girl has that same tangled hair, screaming for a good brushing. She's the one with the *101 Dalmations* bathing suit.

"I'm sorry to bother you," the woman is saying. "But I can't find my little girl. Jessica. The older one?"

Marjorie waits. The woman's hair is the color blond you get when you do it yourself.

"I was on the phone and she wandered off."

"Again!" this little girl blurts. "Mommy says stay in the yard or in the pool and Jessica just doesn't listen."

"Ashley does," the woman says, touching the top of her daughter's head. "But Jessica has a mind of her own."

"Then she lies and says she was right upstairs in her room or something," the little girl adds.

The woman shrugs, a "what are you going to do?" motion that irritates Marjorie. What you're going to do, Marjorie thinks, is watch your children, comb their hair, and stay off the telephone.

"I'm sorry," she says. "I haven't seen her."

"If you do," the woman says, "can you give us a holler?"

"Yes," Marjorie says. "Of course." And they live close enough that a holler would do it too. Disgusted, she closes the door.

THAT NIGHT, THEY still haven't found the little girl. While Marjorie and Gary eat their salads on the patio, they can hear the mother give an anguished description and details to the police, whose car sits in the middle of the street sending a blue light across Marjorie's yard.

"The woman can't keep track of those children," Marjorie tells Gary. "It's no surprise that one has gotten herself lost."

"They're like little ragamuffins," Gary says. He has turned the patio light on himself tonight, and the paper is spread around him like a fairy tale princess's hair. "Little sweet girls," he adds, distracted, turning a page.

Gary is a messy newspaper reader; he turns it all inside

out, pulls the guts of one part away from where it belongs, and leaves the whole thing in disarray. If Marjorie doesn't read it first, she can't piece it back together into a shape that makes sense. She has not read today's yet, and watching Gary tear it apart she knows she won't get a chance now.

Bonnie's news grabs hold of Marjorie. She isn't supposed to tell Gary; Bonnie and Ted want to break the news themselves, in some elaborate manner, at the appropriate time. Bonnie has asked her mother to act surprised when they do. Still, she wants to see Gary's private reaction herself. All day the word *grandmother* has scraped away at Marjorie's insides, eroding pieces of her.

"Gary," she says, her voice low enough to hold a secret.

From behind them, cutting through the kitchen, comes a man's voice.

"Excuse me?" it calls. "Mrs. Macomber?"

Marjorie jumps to her feet, banging her thighs on the sharp metal table. Gary looks at her.

"Probably the police," he says, calmly. "Canvassing the neighborhood."

Marjorie remembers how the garden boy, Justin, stood so long by the fence that morning.

Gary has stood too, to answer the door. But Marjorie grabs him by the arm, hard.

"That boy you hired," she hisses. "Justin. He was up to something over by their yard." She indicates with a tilt of her head so there's no confusing what yard she means.

"By the flower bed, you mean?" Gary says.

"No," she whispers.

The policemen are knocking, banging the M shaped knocker against the door with an urgent desperation.

"I think he was masturbating," she tells Gary. Is that what she had thought? she wonders.

Gary laughs. "Marjorie," he says, in that same affectionate way that seems, now, condescending.

Marjorie remembers how long he stood there, his arms jerking about. She remembers the way he shuddered before he moved on.

"I'm telling you," she says.

But Gary is shaking his head, laughing to himself, heading toward the door.

By the time she joins him, he has already assured the policeman they have not seen the little girl. He is shaking the policeman's hand.

Another policeman comes heavily up the front walk.

"Joe," he says, "we got her. She's been in the garage all day. Hiding."

"Jesus," the first one says. He looks at Gary. "Sorry to bother you."

"They don't watch that child," Marjorie blurts.

She is, oddly, relieved that the little girl has been found. Maybe Justin was just weeding over there. Her own imagination seems enormous, out of control.

"She says she was scared to come out," the second policeman says. "Won't say what she's scared *of*. Just that she's scared."

"They probably watch horribly scary things," Marjorie tells them, even though no one seems to be paying her any attention. "*Jurassic Park* and things of that nature. She's just a little girl."

"Yes, ma'am," they both say, as if it's something they learn in the police academy.

Gary and Marjorie stand on the front steps and watch them get back in their police car, its blue light spinning silently.

"Remember that sweet little doll Bonnie had?" Gary says. "It wore a ragged sort of dress made of burlap? And it had a big tear stuck to its cheek?"

"Little Miss No Name," Marjorie says.

She can't imagine why Gary would remember that doll of Bonnie's, or any doll, for that matter. He hardly seemed to notice Bonnie when she was a little girl. He was too busy then, trying to earn money, to make a name for himself at the insurance company where he now holds the largest office, the corner one with its own cubicle for a secretary, its wide view of things below.

"Yes," Gary says, closing the door. "Those little girls remind me of that doll. Unkempt but lovable."

"Really?" Marjorie says, surprised. "They aren't lovable at all to me."

"MRS. MACOMBER?" Justin says.

He has a way of appearing behind her, out of nowhere, and frightening her. It is very hot today, and humid. He is covered with a shiny layer of sweat, and standing close enough that his smell seems to cling to Marjorie.

"I can't find the gasoline, for the mower. Maybe you're out?"

Marjorie sighs. She has left the cool comfort of central air conditioning inside just long enough to get in her car and drive to the pool at the club. All she has on is a navy blue shift dress, her bathing suit underneath, and sandals. She doesn't want to get all hot and sweaty rummaging through the garage.

"Well," she says, "did you root around inside?" She motions toward the garage behind them. Between them, the hot air ripples. What was it Bonnie said he looked like? A god? Dizzy from the heat, Marjorie can agree. But he smells so ungodly, so earthbound. She wishes he would wear a shirt, at least.

"That's how I know you're out," he says, cocky.

She can't imagine Gary would let something like this happen. It's his job to take care of things like gasoline for the lawn mower, and oil changes for both cars. And hiring gardeners, she adds, turning around and going into the cool dark of the garage. She never comes in here. It smells like metal and fuel, a smell that tastes metallic on her tongue. The light has to be turned on by a string that hangs from a bulb somewhere; she can't find it.

But the boy has followed her inside and says, "It's supposed to be over here."

Instead of searching for the light, Marjorie follows him to one distant corner. She wonders if she's ruining her sandals, getting motor oil on them.

"See for yourself," he says.

She pokes around, among mulch and watering cans and a garden hose coiled up like a snake.

"Hey," the boy says. "Boss."

She turns and he is right up behind her in that way he has. Marjorie feels a dull throb in her groin. This is so cliché, she thinks. She wonders what he expects from her. Is he stupid enough to believe she will grab him and take him right here? But as she thinks it she feels a quiver in her thighs, high up.

"You're a stupid arrogant boy," she says.

He laughs and moves right up to her, pressing her lightly into the bags of mulch. The garden hose is hard against her shins.

"Lady," Justin says, not even bothering to whisper. "You drive me nuts. I mean, I know you're probably even older than my mother, but the way you lay out there all greased up, with that flat stomach and those gorgeous tits, I'm about to go crazy."

Is this really me he's talking about? Marjorie thinks, excited by the idea that a boy who looks like this boy would think of her this way.

"I'm going to be a grandmother," she says.

It is the first time she has ever spoken to him in such a voice, inviting and honest. She imagines she has not used this voice in years, since she was a girl not much older than him, before all the things that happen to a person had happened.

"No shit," Justin says, and lets out a low whistle.

Marjorie reaches up and pulls out the rubber band that hold his dark hair in its ponytail. His hair spills out around him like a girl's.

"Can I touch you?" he says.

She is surprised he asks; his boldness and confidence imply that he just takes what he wants.

As if someone else is controlling her movements, Marjorie takes his hand and moves it under her shift, inside her bathing suit, to where she is hot and wet.

He moans.

Is it possible that she still has this kind of power over someone so young and beautiful? His fingers, rough from garden work, slip inside her and move in the right way. She wonders how many girls he has had, so young.

When Marjorie was in high school and college she believed her virginity was a precious thing, and she held on to it until she and Gary were properly engaged, the wedding date set, everything official. What she did in those days—and what she has not done since—was to take boys into her mouth, feel them swell and push and then burst with come that she used to drink up.

It had seemed back then, groping in cars, burning for sex—her too! she had wanted it as badly as she wants this boy now—that taking them in her mouth was a less intimate act than the real one. That it was somehow all right; that it didn't count. And even though now she knows better, knows it is much more intimate to swallow someone's come, that it does, indeed, count, she kneels on top of the coiled hose and unzips Justin's cutoff jeans—no underwear! His penis springs out at her, beautiful, young, hard. A pale blue vein pulsates across the length of it; Marjorie takes all of him in her mouth, and it is as if she is a young girl herself, a teenager in someone's white Impala, kneeling on the dusty floor, swallowing every inch of them.

Justin comes in such a loud burst, shooting warm come into her mouth, grasping her head between his hands so that he is even deeper, forcing his come down her throat. It is bitter, lovely. When he finally slides from her mouth, he kneels too, on the hard cold floor, and kisses her for the first time, as gentle as a baby.

⌒

BONNIE AND TED have invited them for dinner. This is the night, Marjorie supposes, that Bonnie will tell them the good news. But ever since the morning she first went into the garage with Justin six weeks ago, Marjorie has felt disembodied. She waits for him to arrive on Wednesday and Saturday mornings; she watches from the little window over the kitchen sink as he weeds and clips and mows. By the time he arrives she is all ready for him—a dress, her sandals, and nothing underneath. Marjorie is forty-nine years old and she has never done anything like this. She has been a faithful wife, a good mother, a friend and neighbor others rely on. As summer wears on, she has even helped the woman next door, now almost obscenely pregnant, search for this oldest daughter, Jessica, who hides in small places and will not talk.

Still she meets Justin in the garage, goes to the dark cold corner, and does things with him that she has not done since she was young. She and Gary, who always have had a good solid sex life—even now, married twenty-seven years, they make love once or twice a week. Even now, there are surprises, like that night on the patio.

But there is nothing like this, with this boy, except what she had when she was young and passionate, the hands everywhere, in and out of holes, the desperate licking, as if they could actually literally devour each other. And then, *this* Saturday morning, she finally took him inside her house and inside her, right upstairs on Bonnie's childhood bed, with the white eyelet spread bought at Bloomingdale's, and the frilled canopy that made Bonnie believe she might be a princess.

And now here is Marjorie, in her navy blue summer slacks and striped boat neck cotton sweater, her crotch filled with the ache that good long sex leaves with you, sitting in her daughter's living room at the beach house with an ice cold martini, chewing on cashews, listening to Gary and Ted discuss their morning golf game. She had forgotten what young boys were like, how they stayed hard so long, and could make love twice in the same morning, growing hard again so quickly.

"How is that gorgeous thing?" Bonnie asks Marjorie.

Marjorie holds her breath.

"That god that Daddy hired for the yard," Bonnie says.

"He's off to college," Gary answers. "Phong's son is going to take over next week."

"But that can't be," Marjorie says, with too much enthusiasm so that they are all staring at her, confused. "I mean," she stammers, "he isn't bright enough for college."

Gary shrugs. "Just the state school. But he'll be living there. Besides, you don't like him. Mother thinks he's going to steal something. Or murder us."

Ted and Gary laugh, but Bonnie is studying her mother's face and frowning. Marjorie recognizes the bloated blotchy skin of early pregnancy.

"I think Mother has a crush on this boy," Bonnie says finally. She eats the olive out of Ted's martini and sits back, self-satisfied.

"Absolutely," Marjorie says, coolly. "Every morning when he's finished with his work, I take him inside and make love to him until Daddy pulls up from golf. He's delicious actually."

Only Gary laughs. "That's a good one, old girl," he says, slapping her knee.

Ted and Bonnie look at each other, embarrassed.

Then Ted refills all the drinks and stands, raising his own martini glass, his initials TBC etched into it, and says, "Well, then. It seems time for a toast."

He's practically bursting with his news. Marjorie feels smug, satisfied. She already knows their news, and she has secrets of her own. Good ones, she thinks, still feeling the sting of Gary's playful slap.

"A toast," Ted says, "to the new, about to be grandparents."

Gary looks shocked. His cheeks redden. "My God," he says, then shakes Ted's hand with ridiculous enthusiasm, as if, Marjorie thinks, fucking is something to be congratulated.

"Here's to me then," she says. At first, downing the cold martini, she is smiling at her own little joke. But suddenly, from nowhere, she finds herself crying. Sobbing, really. Unable to stop, to catch her breath, to do anything but stand there and cry.

MARJORIE DOES THE unthinkable. She waits for Justin to come loping up the street and, before he can disappear into the garage to get the lawn mower, she calls him inside, in a too loud voice—those new people seem to be everywhere, all the time.

"Justin!" Marjorie says. "I need some help with the air conditioning system. It's making an odd noise."

He stands at the foot of the driveway, thumbs hooked in his cutoffs' pockets, smirking.

"Really?" he says. "I'm not very good with electrical stuff." He speaks loudly too.

In high school, Marjorie was an actress, the star of all the school plays—*Our Town* and *A Streetcar Named Desire* and, in her senior year, *The Children's Hour.* She has forgotten how that felt, to be on stage, to be watched, until right now.

"I'm hot," she announces. "It can't wait."

And then she does the really unthinkable. Marjorie leads him into *her* room, hers and Gary's, onto *their* bed. The room is, she realizes as Justin stands naked in the middle of it, stuffy and imposing. The smell of peach potpourri hangs in the air with its false aroma, not at all reminiscent of peaches. It's the room of two old people. Marjorie sees that now.

But Justin is on her, with his sex talk, dirty and guttural in a way that no one has ever spoken to her.

"Give me that pussy," he says. "Fuck me."

And later he tells her that her tits are fantastic, that she tastes so good, that her ass drives him nuts. The talk does something to her, to *them,* because even though the clock—a silly old lady clock from a long ago trip to Germany, Switzerland, and Austria—is inching toward noon, when Gary gets back from golf and late morning martinis, Marjorie is back on Justin, frantically pulling him into her.

The voice that floats up from downstairs—"*Mrs. Macomber? You home?*"—frightens Marjorie so much that she yelps, and thinks for a moment she might faint.

"*Mrs. Macomber?*"

Marjorie grabs her robe, pulls it on, and races downstairs where, standing in the foyer, is the mother from next door.

"I'm sorry to bother you," the woman says, frowning.

Her maternity top, pink with blue giraffes bouncing across her grossly large belly, is pulled tight.

Marjorie knows what she's thinking, how odd it is for someone like Marjorie to be still in her robe this late in the morning. Is she thinking too that the garden boy has come in and never gone back out? The lawn is unmowed, the hedges unclipped. Dandelions poke their heads out here and there.

"I was getting into the shower," Marjorie says.

A thin stream of come trickles out of her, down her thigh, and she pushes her legs together.

"It's just Jessica again," the woman says, arms open in apology. "Except this time she took Ashley with her."

"You know she hides in the garage," Marjorie says.

The grandfather's clock chimes noon; Gary could walk in right now. Upstairs, Justin is naked, hard, waiting. And more than anything, that is where Marjorie wants to be too, with that boy, in his tattooed arms, feeling his long hair on her breasts. For a crazy moment, Marjorie thinks she will run off with him. She will leave everything and go with this boy somewhere.

Annoyed, Marjorie says, "Have you looked in the garage?"

The woman blushes and nods.

"It's just so hard for me to get around," she explains. "And it's so hot out." Then she looks at Marjorie, expressionless, and says, "It ain't hot in here, though. Is it?"

Marjorie meets her gaze. Beneath the pink silk of her robe, she feels her heart fluttering like a butterfly trapped in a jar.

"Let me get dressed," she says finally.

The woman smiles a broad smile that shows all her small teeth.

Marjorie was right; Justin is still on her bed, stretched out naked, stroking his penis.

"You have to get dressed," she says, turning her back to him as she takes off the robe and slips on a beige cotton sift.

"Not until you come here and sit on this," he says.

Everything seems to be off balance, Marjorie thinks. Because she is afraid the woman knows, and she is afraid that Gary will walk in, and yet she takes the shift back off and does what Justin asks and, riding him, she imagines again that she will leave here with him, that they will just do this, somewhere, anywhere.

When they are both done, toppled over him, she says, "You didn't say you were leaving. Going to college." Saying it, she feels as betrayed as she did when her high school boyfriend—a year older—left her behind to go off to Yale.

"Yeah," he says, his fingers tangled in her hair. "Well."

Marjorie sits up, looks down at him, at the sweaty curled hair that climbs down his chest and belly, and his penis lying pink and soft, pointing lazily upward.

"We could go away together," she says.

"Like to the beach or something?" he asks her, puzzled.

"No," Marjorie tells him. "Really away. Run off."

Justin laughs. "You're crazy," he says.

But he is happy with the idea. She can tell by the way he pulls her back down to kiss her, fully, on her bruised lips.

BY THE TIME Marjorie appears next door, the girls have been found. They make themselves small, roll into tight balls, like a Persian cat Marjorie once had. She stands in the open garage door, where their mother kneels before them. Both girls are sucking their thumbs. The younger one has her eyes closed, and she rocks back and forth like she is trying to soothe herself, to go to sleep.

"I knew they were okay," Marjorie announces. Her voice is bright; maybe tomorrow or the day after she will be gone.

The mother turns toward her. "But they say they're not," she tells Marjorie.

Marjorie is impatient with this woman, who clutters the neighborhood, the O'Haras' yard, with *Lion King* swimming pools and lost children, who has babies she can't take care of, and expects everyone to give her a hand.

"But here they are," Marjorie says. "Fine." Actually, they don't *look* fine. They look frightened or even a little crazy.

The older one says, talking around her thumb, "The boogeyman got me again."

The younger girl nods, eyes still closed, rocking back and forth.

Their mother gets to her feet with some difficulty. "That's what I've been hearing all fucking summer."

Her language, out here on a bright summer day, shocks Marjorie.

"The boogeyman, the boogeyman. They say he comes in here and gets them. First it was just Jessica. Now Ashley's starting too."

"He's hairy! And he's ugly!" Ashley blurts. "And he hurts us!" She runs past her mother and Marjorie, into the house.

The older girl says solemnly, "He has a big long thing, like a dragon has maybe, and he makes us touch it and today he put it in my mouth until fire came out."

Of course it's the girl's imagination talking. Marjorie can't believe it's anything else.

"My God," the mother says. "What is she telling me?" The woman looks to Marjorie and asks again. "What is she saying?"

WHEN GARY GETS home it is after two, and he has had too many martinis.

"I'm drunk," he says happily. "God, it's good to get drunk in the middle of the day." He is red-faced and red-eyed.

Marjorie has put her robe back on and is sitting in the cool dark of the family room. She is almost happy for her husband's drunkenness; she has not showered away all of the sex she had that morning, she has not made the bed. She has simply sat here, trying to piece together what is going on. Gnawing at her is that she was right all along; something is very wrong with Justin. He has done something to those little girls. But when? she keeps thinking. She watched him come up the street. And she reminds herself how the older girl is a liar; someone has said that.

Sloppily, Gary makes room for himself on the chair where she sits. He licks her neck. When she pulls away, he says, "I'm probably too damn drunk anyway."

She doesn't know why she brings it up, but she says, "There's something going on next door. With those children."

Gary buries his head in her chest and murmurs, "Why,

you smell funny! All sweaty! Where's your kiwi soap and your grapefruit bubblebath? You smell like you've been in the hot yard."

Marjorie tries to pull away, but he holds on too tight. She says, "You don't think Justin would do anything to those girls, do you?" She laughs when she says it out loud. "That's ridiculous," she says. "I know it is." Somehow, she does know it. They have told themselves ghost stories, the way children do, and frightened each other. They need friends. They need to go to day camp somewhere and make bracelets out of gimp and eat s'mores.

"Oh," Gary says, "those beautiful delicate little things. That one, that littlest one, has yellow in her eyes, like that old tabby we used to have. She is the prettier one, I think." He climbs onto Marjorie's lap, awkward and drunk, smelling of booze, and wraps his arms around her. "I wish I could," he mutters, resting his head on her shoulders, "but I'm too drunk and tired and old. Probably in this condition, that gardener you like so little could still manage. But I'm a grandfather, after all."

Marjorie cannot get her own arms around him, so they sit there, like that, for too long, in the cool, dim room.

IT IS LATER that night, as Marjorie stands over the hot stove frying bacon for a bacon and egg supper, that Gary, head aching, breath sour, says: "I'm so ashamed."

The bacon hisses and splatters Marjorie's arm, burning her.

"It's just that I told them our news, about Bonnie and the baby coming, and they kept toasting me, buying more drinks." Gary stares into his cup of black coffee. "It's humiliating really."

Marjorie takes the bacon from the pan and lays it to drain on paper towels decorated with homespun advice: *Home is where the heart is. There's no place like home. Friends and family matter most.* She cracks eggs, four of them, right into the hot bacon grease. This is what makes the best fried eggs, she knows.

As they cook, she studies them, the way the white part bleeds and the yolk clots.

"How do you know about that girl's eyes?" Marjorie says.

"What girl?" Gary asks, and Marjorie hears the chair squeak across the floor as he sits up straighter.

"The little one next door. Ashley." She prods at the eggs with a spatula, letting the hot grease seep beneath them.

"I don't know about her eyes," Gary says. "Those poor little things," he adds, changing the direction. "No one tends them at all. They smell sour, you know."

Their faces float above the heat that rises from the frying pan, the snarled hair and frightened faces.

"They're just children," Marjorie says, her voice flat and even. "Little girls."

Gary doesn't answer. When she finally turns to face him, he has his face buried in his hands. She watches his shoulders shaking, sees the bright red of a flush creep across his forehead and scalp. Outside, the automatic timer sends light across the patio and the ragged lawn. Beyond it, Marjorie can see the sloped roof of the new people's house, where inside those little girls are doing what—cowering? hiding? telling everything? Smoke rises from the burning grease and eggs, foul.

Marjorie stumbles to the sliding glass door and yanks it open. She steps onto the patio, its stones cold on her bare feet, and she keeps walking. The grass—twice now she has kept Justin from doing what he came here to do—is wet and scratchy on her ankles.

She goes to the garage and takes the mower from its place, and pushes it out to the yard. It spits, then turns on, and Marjorie uses all her strength, everything, to push it in a zigzag line across her yard, cutting away the weeds and grass. Funny how the yard looks so flat until you do this, until you push this way; then you see how uphill it really is. She mows and mows, unable to put her thoughts in any order that makes sense. The timer shuts off, leaving just her kitchen illuminated, with her husband sitting at the table, unmoving, a distinguished man with silver hair.

In the darkness, Marjorie chews up flowers, fallen twigs. When the silent blue light from a police car spins across her old, stately yard, she keeps going. They are outside her house, those policemen. They are about to come in.

AN ORNITHOLOGIST'S

GUIDE TO LIFE

ALL OF THE HOUSES on our street were in some form of disrepair. This was Park Slope, Brooklyn, 1974. This was the land of brownstones to be had for next to nothing. Crumbling, linoleumed, shag carpeted, knotty oak paneled brownstones. They held the promise of hidden treasures in the form of parquet floors and intricately tiled fireplaces. At dinner parties, my parents and their friends talked endlessly about what they had uncovered. The spring the Bishops arrived, the biggest find belonged to the Markowitzes: an entire staircase, small and steep and painted sea green. We speculated about the slave trade, prostitution, homosexual love. But the Markowitzes only gloated, happy to unseat the Randalls who had discovered an entire stained-glass window that winter. Cracked and missing pieces, it still stood as a majestic tribute to everyone's wisdom in leaving Manhattan with its crime and high rents and small apartments for Brooklyn, the New Frontier.

I was eleven going on twelve that year the Bishops moved across the street from us. I had bad tonsils. They had to come out. But every time my surgery date neared I got another bout of tonsillitis. By March I had missed fifty-two days of school and developed an allergy to penicillin. To keep me occupied—our family was in a no television phase then—my father gave me a guidebook to birds and a pair of binoculars. "Open your eyes, Alice," he told me, "to the exciting world of ornithology." Then he went off to work.

The year before he had told me, "Everybody talks about the weather, Alice. But nobody does anything about it." For a while I measured rainfall and hours of sunlight and tracked the highest and lowest temperatures around the world. But then the tonsillitis began and I abandoned meteorology. Ornithology could be practiced from my bed, if necessary, though on good days I walked the four blocks to Prospect Park in hopes of an exciting discovery.

From my room, I could gaze out the bay window and into the treetops. Beyond the treetops I could see the Bishops' house, perfectly. Since the variety of birds in Brooklyn was small—sparrows, robins, and finches mostly—watching the Bishops was at least equally as interesting.

The day they moved in, a cold and rainy March day, I was home with a new bout of sore tonsils, eating blue Popsicles and hoping for a cardinal sighting. Instead, I saw the U-Haul truck pull up and the Bishops emerge, blinking and dazed like they had landed on the moon. All of them looked misplaced, even the father, who lacked the efficient demeanor of most of the fathers I knew. Mr. Bishop appeared to have just woken up. Mrs. Bishop seemed about to break, too delicate and fragile for a mother. Normally I would have delighted in spying on two girls moving into our neighborhood, but these two, shivering in their thin cotton shirts and jeans jackets, wispy blond hair tangling in the rain, did not look like new friends to me.

Just-beginning-to-bud trees blocked the view between the street and the Bishops' third floor. Disappointed, I turned my attention back to birdwatching. "The only essential equipment for seeing birds is a pair of eyes," my guidebook said. I ate blue Popsicles and chewed Aspergum. Our house filled with the sounds of repair, drills, saws, large things being torn apart. I watched.

"THE PHOEBE," MY mother, Phoebe, announced drunkenly, "is the only bird who says its name."

We were hosting the welcome party for the Bishops. All the parties in those days were the same. Vats of vegetarian food—hummus and lasagna and tabouleh. Down on Atlantic Avenue Middle Eastern stores lined the street and supplied our neighborhood with all of its hors d'ouevres. The adults drank jugs of chianti, talked too loudly, burned thick candles everywhere, played old Bob Dylan albums, sang Simon and Garfunkel songs until their voices cracked. The Bishops didn't know what to make of any of it.

"It's true," my mother insisted. "The phoebe is unique that way."

Mr. Bishop, who had been aloof and maybe even bored the entire night, said suddenly and loudly, "Bobwhite! Bobwhite!" He said it like a challenge, in a booming voice.

My mother laughed. "Excuse me?" she said. Whenever she drank too much wine she grew an accent like the Queen of England.

"The bobwhite, darling," Mr. Bishop said, leaning his tall frame until his face was very close to hers. "The bobwhite says its name."

Of course everyone was watching. Already no one much liked the Bishops. He drank scotch all night and refused the lasagna; he was a playwright who had come here from California. His wife had murder in her past, which explained the terrified look she wore. Her entire family—parents and two brothers—had been famously killed while they slept in their suburban Ohio home; Mrs. Bishop was away at college. She was an artist of some kind, a dancer or a poet, mysterious and sad. Mr. Bishop, Colin, was tall and hawk-nosed but his wife was small and slender with thick wavy blond hair. Her name was Babe.

"They're quails, you know," Mr. Bishop told my mother as if he were sharing a great confidence.

From where I sat, bored and sleepy, my throat still aching, on our brown corduroy beanbag, I could see that Mr. Bishop had one ear pierced and wore a diamond stud in it.

"Honestly," my mother said, all la-di-dah, "I don't know one fucking thing about birds."

Mr. Bishop thought this was the funniest thing ever. He laughed long and hard, still way too close to my mother, who smiled up at him.

"Do you know anything about stained-glass windows?" Mrs. Randall was asking Mrs. Bishop. That's how Mrs. Randall was, relentless. At her house she never left you alone, always plying you with her homemade granola or iced tea with soggy mint leaves floating in it. "Because I believe this one could be a Tiffany. An original. The amethyst and topaz colors are as rich as any I've seen in the books. Maybe you could come and look at it? Maybe tomorrow?"

"I don't know," Mrs. Bishop said, trying to catch her husband's attention. But he only had eyes for my mother. He had knelt down at her side and the two of them, heads bent toward each other, were talking quietly.

"I won't hold you to it," Mrs. Randall said. "Just a look-see."

My father stood in the corner with two other men who also worked in Manhattan. He went off to teach Earth Science at City College; Mr. Randall was in advertising, like Darren on *Bewitched,* and he had the same buggy eyes and nervous sweaty look about him as Darren; Mr. Markowitz worked in book publishing and liked to toss around the names of writers everyone was supposed to have read but who my mother always dismissed as schlocky. Whenever they got together, which was almost every weekend, after they discussed grouting and wholesale tile warehouses, they talked about how wonderful Brooklyn was, as if they were trying to convince each other that was true.

The walls in this room were streaked at least a dozen different colors, from beige to buttercream. We were living with them to see which one suited us before we painted the room. My father stood in front of the lightest streaks, the beige and ivory and antique white. But my mother and Mr. Bishop were nearest the bright yellows, the ones we had already discarded as silly. Yet that night, at least from where I sat, those yellows seemed to illuminate my mother's face, to cast a light, in fact, around the two of them.

"BIRDS ARE GROUPED into orders, families, and genera according to similarities of bills, feet, and internal anatomy," my guidebook said. "If you know these groups, the relationship and classification of birds will be clearer." So I set about memorizing the groups. Herons and bitterns; plovers and snipes; hummingbirds and woodpeckers; hawks, eagles, and vultures. I liked to memorize things. I knew every birthstone for every month, for example, and pestered people to quiz me. My mother didn't usually indulge me. But my father would happily ask, "August?" and beam when I answered, "Peridot." I knew the birthdays of rock stars, the dates famous people died in plane crashes (Jim Croce, Carole Lombard, Glenn Miller), the dates and personality characteristics of every astrological sign.

"Your scientific name," I told my mother, "is *Sayornis phoebe.*"

"Great," she said. "Terrific." She was working on plans for a porch. My father did not pay attention to her desire for a porch in the back of the house. *We need plumbing*, he would say. *We need electricity on the third floor. We need to fix the goddamn holes in the walls and all you can think about is a porch?*

Finally, spring had arrived with thick hot air and too-bright sunshine. In our curtainless kitchen, all that light made everything seem even worse than it was. The old appliances sat away from the walls, unplugged and uncleaned. Half of the linoleum was curled back, exposing not a lovely hardwood floor but speckled concrete. We were in the process of tearing down two walls, which left every surface covered with a thin veneer of plaster. For the next two weeks, we were eating only cold food or take-out.

For lunch, my mother had opened a bag of Fritos and a can of deviled ham. The Fritos hurt my throat. My new tonsillectomy date was May 4, in just ten days. My mother had ordered me to stay healthy.

"Do you know the scientific name for a blue jay?" I asked my mother.

She kept drawing. "Honey," she said, "I don't care." Even though she had quit smoking years earlier, she had very recently started up again. But she lit cigarettes and then seemed to forget she was a smoker, leaving them to burn on the edge of the kitchen sink or in one of the shells we'd brought home from our vacation in Cape May last summer. A curl of smoke from her forgotten Salem drifted in front of her.

"*Cyanocitta cristata,*" I told her.

She looked up, as if she had just realized I was there. "I forgot," she said. "We're having dinner at the Bishops' tonight. Just us. Colin doesn't like big neighborhood things." She noticed her cigarette then and took a halfhearted puff. "Oh," she said. "Maybe you can make friends with the daughters. I think they're lonely."

"They wear flip-flops to school," I said.

She smiled. "Do they? Is that allowed?"

"Everything's allowed," I mumbled. My school was a progressive cooperative school, which meant parents were always lurking around and we spent more time expressing ourselves than learning real school things. We baked bread and kept a sad little vegetable garden, we cooked spaghetti on Fridays and dressed in traditional Vietnam folk costumes to celebrate Tet. Flip-flops were not going to cause much of a stir there. I changed tactics. "Fiona smokes pot," I said.

My mother laughed. "What is she? Thirteen? Please, Alice. Don't be so dramatic."

"*Colinus virginianus,*" I said.

"What?"

"That's the bobwhite," I said, waiting for a reaction. But she was already gone, back to her dreams of a porch.

IN SOME WAYS, Brooklyn was exciting. For one thing, we had a yard. For another, suspicious-looking people roamed the periphery of the streets, adding a sense of danger that had been missing on West Twelfth Street. As for birds, however, Brooklyn was disappointing. Still, I sat, binoculars in hand, watching and waiting for a discovery. Through the pink and white blossoms of the dogwood trees, planted by the Neighborhood Association, I could just make out the Bishops' second floor. Mrs. Bishop was painting there. All day she painted. I could see the tumble of her blond hair, the motion of her arms as she worked.

Mr. Bishop slept. He was in Manhattan at rehearsals of his play until late into the night. Sometimes I heard a taxi door slam and I would open my eyes to see the silver light of dawn covering our street. His play was done in the nude by three naked actors sitting on the edge of a Dumpster. It was about politics and ideas. No one understood any of it, although my mother had announced that Colin Bishop was a genius.

I watched a robin tend her three perfect blue ovals of eggs.

Beyond the nest, I saw Mr. Bishop, shirtless, in the kitchen, finally awake. It was four o'clock in the afternoon. My father left the house at six-thirty in the morning, smelling of Irish Spring soap and shoe polish. He returned twelve hours later. I could set a watch by my father's comings and goings. He was predictable, someone a person could count on. I knew that at seven o'clock he watched the news with Roger Grimsby and drank a Heineken straight out of its green bottle. I knew that he read *Time* magazine in the bathroom, keeping them neatly stacked on the back of the toilet where they would wrinkle from dampness. I knew that on Saturday mornings he jogged around Prospect Park even if it was raining or freezing or humid and hot. He came home with bagels and orange juice and the newspaper; I could rely on that.

But what about a person like Mr. Bishop? A person who stayed out all night with naked people sitting on Dumpsters in warehouses south of Houston Street? A person who slept all day and walked around the house naked maybe? He was a person with no roots. He had migrated here from California via Chicago and Minneapolis and who knew where else. What could Fiona and Imogen depend on him for? What could Mrs. Bishop rely on? The ground beneath their brownstone seemed shaky to me. No matter how much Mrs. Bishop painted, I wondered what she could possibly hope for in the end.

MY FATHER BROUGHT a dark green box with a gold bow on top to dinner at the Bishops' that night.

"How does he afford this stuff?" he mumbled as we crossed the street. "It's pretentious, if you want to ask me."

My mother rolled her eyes and smoothed her skirt. My father hated that skirt, a long thing with rows of different material. He thought she looked silly in it. She hated his bow ties. *My students get a kick out of them,* he told her. If I closed my eyes I could recite the order of the fabric: red and yellow flowers, black corduroy, green and gold paisley, denim, blue and white boat striped, and then a final black velvet ruffle. She always wore it with a white pocket tee shirt tucked into the waist, and a fat belt of large silver discs connected by rope.

"Why did you wear that thing?" my father said. He didn't expect an answer. He rang the doorbell and stared hard at the front door, which had been stripped of paint and stood bare before us.

Fiona opened the door. She was stoned, even I knew that, and I'd only had two of the required drug education classes at school. Her eyes were heavy lidded and she wore a stupid grin. Also, she smelled of pot. In our school, the playground was a drug paradise, with pills and hashish and pot getting traded the way the younger kids traded baseball cards.

"Hey," she said, and smiled at us. Fiona's teeth were beautiful and white and straight. The boys all loved her, with those teeth and that pale blond hair.

We followed her through a labyrinth of empty rooms to the kitchen. Unlike everyone else we knew, the Bishops had done their kitchen first, and after the chipped paint and scuffed floors we'd passed on our way, the kitchen positively dazzled us. A double slate sink. Marble floor. A library table set with dishes the color of dangerous things like maraschino cherries and orange nuclear waste. At the six burner Glenwood stove, stirring and tasting, stood not Mrs. Bishop, but Mr. Bishop. I had never seen my father cook anything. My mother even grilled the hamburgers and hot dogs in the summer. But Mr. Bishop looked relaxed and in charge. He was drinking wine from a water glass and when he saw us, after he shook hands with my father and hugged my mother, he poured them each a glass too.

My mother elbowed me toward Fiona, who was staring at us blankly.

"Why don't you show Alice around?" she said to Fiona. "I know she'd like to see your room."

I groaned.

"Okay," Fiona said in her placid voice.

The kitchen was warm and smelled of garlic and exotic spices. I didn't want to leave it. But I once again followed Fiona, this time upstairs to her room. Instead of a door, a curtain of beads hung in the doorway. She parted it for me and then flopped onto her bed, which was really just a mattress on the floor, covered with Indian bedspreads.

"You like Jethro Tull?" she said, putting the arm down on an album before I could answer. *"Aqualung,"* she said. She sighed. "We won't be here long. We just sort of, you know." She moved her hands like a hula dancer and smiled to herself. "Pass through. Usually my father does something terrible and there's some kind of scene." She squinted up at me. "I bet your father never makes a scene."

"I don't know," I said, shrugging.

"I bet your mother does though. Right?" before I could answer she said, "Isn't this flute like so, I don't know?"

Then she closed her eyes and moved her head in time with the music.

I listened but I didn't like the music. There was nothing

to look at in the room. No posters on the wall. No place for me to sit, unless I climbed on the mattress beside Fiona, which seemed uncool. I stood awkwardly by the curtain of beads, until I realized that Fiona had actually drifted off to sleep. Her breathing was slow and even. "Fiona?" I said softly. But she didn't wake up.

As quietly as I could, I moved between the beads and out into the hallway. Leaning against the wall were framed posters from museum shows in London and Los Angeles and Chicago. All the doors were shut except for one room where the door was off its hinges and propped at an odd angle in the frame. I stepped inside.

Mrs. Bishop was in there painting. This was the room I could see from my bedroom and now I saw what was taking her so long. She was painting a mural that spread across all four walls, a mural of a garden filled with bright flowers— asters and zinnias and dahlias and marigolds—all of them thick with paint and color, oranges and yellows and purples and reds.

She didn't stop painting when I walked in. She said, "Oh? Is it dinner already?"

"I don't know," I said. "I was just looking around."

"Find anything interesting?" she said. She was working on a section of tulips.

"This is pretty interesting," I said.

"I always paint a garden in a new house. Always," she said.

I nodded. I was thinking about birds, how their bills developed depending on the food they ate. The shrike, the cardinal, the wood thrush, the crossbill, the yellow throat were all in the same family, yet their bills all looked different.

Mrs. Bishop looked up then and smiled. Her teeth were

horsey and big, but they only added to her unique look. "I guess we should see what's cooking, hmmm?"

My mother would have showered and primped before joining her guests. But Mrs. Bishop didn't bother. She stayed in her paint splattered clothes, her hair in a messy ponytail, without even bothering to put on shoes. When we walked into the kitchen, my mother smiled her Queen Elizabeth smile.

"Babe," she said. "I was wondering where you were."

My father sat at the table eating olives and looking miserable.

"Upstairs," Mrs. Bishop said.

"She'll have to show you her masterpiece sometime," Mr. Bishop said.

I wanted to say that it was beautiful. But something stopped me. Perhaps it was the way Mr. Bishop had said the word *masterpiece*. Or the way my mother smiled when he did. Or maybe it was just the air in the kitchen that night, which seemed oddly charged, the way the air feels just before a cold front moves in.

ONE DAY TO my tonsillectomy and I spiked a fever during School Meeting. In School Meeting, all the sixth, seventh, and eighth graders sat on colorful cushions in the Activity Room and aired our feelings. Susan Markowitz wanted to talk about male chauvinism, how the boys dominated certain areas of the school. Trini Randall wanted to discuss changing the morning snack from peanut butter and crackers to fruit and nuts. Fiona Bishop used her red cushion as a pillow, stretched out with her head on it, and went to sleep.

I raised my hand.

"Alice?" said Bob, my literature teacher.

"My throat hurts. It feels like I have razor blades in it."

The health teacher, Patty, came over to me and touched my forehead with her large cool hand. "You have a temperature," she said. "Do you want me to call your mom?"

"I'll just go home by myself," I said.

"Do you want Trini to walk with you?"

I shook my head. As I gathered my things, I heard Felix Crawley saying that the school should write a letter to the president about the MIAs. Once, at a Saturday night dinner at the Crawleys', I had let Felix French-kiss me. Now his voice made me nauseated. His tongue had felt cold and slimy and ever since I had hated him. With my head hurting and my throat sore, I practically ran out of there and the six blocks home, past the bodega with its weird chicken smells and the Irish bar with its stale beer smell and the head shop with its strong incense and B.O. smell. Finally I was home and all I could think of was a blue Popsicle and TV game shows.

But when I pushed into the kitchen I found my mother and Mr. Bishop eating Chinese food and drinking my father's Heineken.

"Oh, no," my mother said when she saw me. "Not your throat."

She had a smear of brown sauce on her cheek, as if she'd been sticking her whole face in the white cartons of food. When she reached her hand out to touch my forehead, I pulled away.

"What's the matter with her throat?" Mr. Bishop said. He was eating the food with long green chopsticks, and they hung in the air like daggers.

"It's her tonsils," my mother said, exasperated. "She was supposed to finally have them out tomorrow but they can't operate if they're infected." She stood up and sighed. "I'll have to call Dr. Williams again and cancel. Get you some antibiotics."

Mr. Bishop took hold of her wrist. "Phoebe, don't you know that antibiotics are poisoning us? Really they are. Soon they won't even work anymore and new mutant bacteria will kill us all."

She sat back down. He didn't let go of her wrist. "Do you know about the Bach Flower Remedies?"

My mother shook her head. The way she looked at Mr. Bishop made me uncomfortable, like I shouldn't be there. I rummaged in the freezer for a stray Popsicle.

"Dr. Edward Bach discovered them in England in the thirties. Thirty-eight different flowers for various characteristics and emotions. Let me bring some by for Alice tomorrow."

"We're out of Popsicles," I said.

"Yes, bring them," my mother said. "You're absolutely right. The antibiotics aren't doing a thing."

EVERY DAY FOR a week Mr. Bishop arrived at one o'clock with a combination of cherry plum, clematis, impatiens, rock rose, and star of Bethlehem in a vial with an eye dropper. He placed four drops on my tongue while I glared at him through my feverish eyes. "I need medicine," I croaked, my throat worse every day.

After he left I propped my pillows up so I could watch

the mother robin feeding her newly hatched babies. They were ugly, those babies, like Martians. But she tended them carefully, bringing them worms and bugs to eat, flapping her wings whenever she arrived.

Our new stove had arrived. My mother cooked all morning, preparing for Mr. Bishop's visit. I would hear her downstairs in the kitchen, the clanging of lids on pots, the whir of her Cuisinart, the one my father had surprised her with last Christmas. Then strange smells drifted up to my bedroom. Mr. Bishop liked Italian food. Not the kind we ate at Rossini's in the Village, but another kind with no red sauce or melted cheese. She made him a special rice that required her to stand at the stove and stir it constantly, adding small amounts of warm broth at certain intervals. When I called down in my hoarse voice for ginger ale, she answered, "I can't leave the risotto, Alice!" She roasted pork with sprigs of rosemary that looked like part of the robin's nest outside my window. She sautéed sweetbreads, which were not bread at all but rather the internal organs of some animal. The smells made me gag.

So did the drops of rescue remedy that Mr. Bishop administered. My tongue felt swollen and burned by them. He looked solemn afterward.

"Alice," he said each time, "you are on the road to recovery. Wait and see."

Then he'd screw the lid back on the vial and go downstairs where he and my mother ate for hours. I listened to the lilt and murmur of their voices, hating both of them. From my window I watched him leave for the theater, and watched my father walk up our street a few hours later, precisely at six-thirty. My mother served him leftovers, reheated, and sat at the table smoking cigarettes, watching as he ate.

U<small>NBELIEVABLY</small>, I <small>AWOKE</small> one morning a week after Mr. Bishop began treating me with the Bach Flower Remedies, cured. I swallowed easily. I spoke clearly. It was a glorious warm day and the sun was bright and yellow in the sky. My mother had already begun making lunch for Mr. Bishop. She sat at the kitchen table hand-grating from a big wheel of stinky cheese. I slipped out unnoticed, my binoculars around my neck and my birding notebook in my hand.

In school I had done an oral report on ornithology. The topic was "My Hobby." Trini Randall gave a talk on ikebana, the art of Japanese flower arranging. She had taken a class on it at the Botanical Garden. Felix gave his on collecting bottle caps. He had shown a cigar box painted in splatter paint and filled with bottle caps he found on the streets of our neighborhood. But my report was the best because ornithology really was my hobby and I really had started to love it. Unlike meteorology, ornithology taught useful skills. The skills of observation. The powers of deduction.

"Birdwatching is exciting," I'd said, "because birds are easy to see, easy to identify, great in numbers and variety, beautiful to observe, and attractive to hear."

On this May morning, as I walked into Prospect Park, the trill and chirp of various birds filled my ears. I could make out the birds singing each song, the black throated green warbler, the chickadee, and the wood thrush with its clear, flutelike sound. I stood beneath the blooming trees and lifted my face upward where the birds perched high above me.

Something caught my eye. At first, I thought it was a crow. But then I saw its yellow bill. My mind raced through all the birds I had memorized, alphabetically, the red-eyed vireo and scarlet tanager, the northern cardinal and rose-breasted grosbeak. But it was none of these. I was almost certain that I was looking at a yellow-billed magpie, a bird that did not migrate east. I stood staring up at that bird until my neck ached and my fingers gripping the binoculars grew numb. A yellow-billed magpie, I knew, had no reason to be in Brooklyn, New York.

I recorded my observations in my notebook, then slowly made my way home, imagining how I would call my local birdwatching club and report my discovery. Maybe I would even get on the news with Roger Grimsby. I could see myself in Prospect Park, under the trees, getting interviewed live. I could warn the population of Park Slope about the yellow-billed magpie. With its impressive sweeping tail, it was easy to admire. But like its cousin the crow, it could easily become a pest. Roger Grimsby and all of New York City would be impressed by my knowledge.

At my front door I paused. A small bundle of dried grass lay at the foot of the steps. With my toe I lifted the grass and saw that this was the nest I had watched all these weeks. The smallest slivers of blue eggshell still clung in places. But the birds were gone. They had flown away. Carefully, I picked up the nest, unsure of what else to do, and carried it inside with me.

At the grand staircase that led upstairs, I stood still, listening to the voices of my mother and Mr. Bishop from somewhere in the house.

"Pine," he was saying, "to rid you of guilt. Honeysuckle to keep you from living in the past."

I heard this and understood he had brought her a remedy too.

Since we'd moved in here, the house had smelled of paint and plaster, of cottonseed oil and sawdust. But as I stood holding that nest, the air smelled unfamiliar, like the strange Italian food my mother had been cooking and other unfamiliar smells, things I could not identify.

The excitement of my discovery began to fade. Gently, I placed the nest on the bottom step. These stairs had been covered in dark orange indoor outdoor carpeting when we'd moved in. My parents had spent hours on their hands and knees, removing it from the stairs and marveling at the fine wood beneath it. I could still see the circular motion of my mother's hands as she'd nourished the wood, sanding it, then oiling it, until it gleamed like it did now.

I stepped outside, empty handed, and looked up and down the street, at the brownstones that needed repair, every one of them broken in some way. Nothing looked the same to me. I sat on the stoop and waited. Whether for my mother to come out, or my father to turn the corner, I could not say.